LEE

D1513690

www.**rbooks**.co.uk

C016001701

Also by Ben Horton:

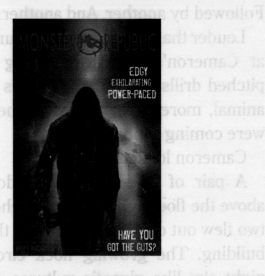

When not writing books, Ben Horton loves directing and acting in plays. His dream is to star in a big-budget Hollywood version of *Monster Republic*. He is a long-time fan of superhero, science fiction and action movies and lives and works in London.

MONSTER REPUBLIC

the judas code

Ben Horton

CORGI BOOKS

MONSTER REPUBLIC: THE JUDAS CODE
A CORGI BOOK 978 0 552 57341 2

Published in Great Britain by Corgi Books,
an imprint of Random House Children's Books
A Random House Group Company

This edition published 2011

1 3 5 7 9 10 8 6 4 2

Copyright © Hothouse Fiction Ltd, 2011
Produced by Hothouse Fiction – www.hothousefiction.com

The Random House Group Limited supports The Forest Stewardship
Council® (FSC®), the leading international forest-certification organisation.
Our books carrying the FSC label are printed on FSC®-certified paper.
FSC is the only forest-certification scheme supported by the leading
environmental organisations, including Greenpeace. Our
paper procurement policy can be found at
www.randomhouse.co.uk/environment

MIX
Paper from
responsible sources
FSC
www.fsc.org   FSC® C018072

Set in Century Old Style

Corgi Books are published by Random House Children's Books,
61–63 Uxbridge Road, London W5 5SA

www.kidsatrandomhouse.co.uk
www.rbooks.co.uk

Addresses for companies within The Random House Group Limited can be
found at: www.randomhouse.co.uk/offices.htm

THE RANDOM HOUSE GROUP Limited Reg. No. 954009

A CIP catalogue record for this book is available from the British Library.

Printed and bound in Great Britain by Clays Ltd, St Ives plc

prologue

'A nation in shock and a party divided. A bitter leadership contest is expected as the Prime Minister resigns, bowing out in the face of an overwhelming vote of no confidence.'

The headlines were read out over footage of the Prime Minister standing in front of the familiar black door of Number Ten Downing Street. Ministers and aides gathered behind him, but he seemed to stand alone against the barrage of camera flashes.

'It is a humiliating defeat for the Prime Minister,' a reporter commented in voice-over, *'who has been under attack from all sides for his failure to prevent last month's terrorist attack at the Broad Harbour memorial service.'*

The picture changed to a shaky hand held shot of a crowd of people fleeing from an explosion under a spreading pall of smoke.

'No group has claimed responsibility for the attack, which struck at the heart of the Broad Harbour community at a time when it was already dealing with the tragic aftermath of an explosion at the local nuclear power plant, but sources who attended the memorial service blame the outrage on a violent local cult calling themselves the "Monster Republic". This secretive group – rumoured to have strong links with foreign terrorist organizations – is also believed to have been behind the original power-plant bombing.'

The camera cut to a shot of a young woman clutching a frightened-looking toddler.

'Everyone knows that Monster Republic did it,' she said, *'but nobody can find them. It's not good enough. No one's safe with scum like that roaming the streets. People can't even let their kids out to play in the park. The government needs to find these monsters, lock them up and throw away the key.'*

The view cut back to the reporter, microphone in hand, in Downing Street.

'Responding to such widespread public criticism, in his last act before he leaves office, the Prime Minister has dispatched a special military task force to Broad Harbour to track down and destroy the elusive cult.'

A montage of pictures showed troops gathered on the Tarmac at an army base, and trucks being loaded with equipment and men.

'According to a Ministry of Defence spokesperson, the task force is already en route to Broad Harbour, and the operation to hunt down the terrorists is to commence immediately. Meanwhile—'

With a whine of hydraulics, a steel foot snapped out into the screen, smashing the TV in a shower of glass and sparks.

Slater turned to Rora with a snarl. 'What now?'

Dr Lazarus Fry switched off his own television with a delicate tap of the remote control. He smiled and gently swirled the brandy around in his glass. Then he raised it in a silent toast to the departing Prime Minister.

The tall, well-built man standing at his shoulder cleared his throat.

'Yes, Hardiman?' prompted Fry, without turning his head. 'What is it?'

'Well, you heard the news, sir. The army is coming. Shouldn't we be making an effort to find the Rejects before they do?'

Fry smiled coldly.

'*The Rejects*,' he said, almost savouring the word, 'are experts at hiding. I sincerely doubt that the army will have any better luck finding them than our own Bloodhounds.'

He fell to thinking, studying the luxurious furnishings of his study, so finely reflected in the blank screen of his television. 'No, I think it's time to kennel the pack and try a new approach.'

'A new approach, sir?'

Fry's smile spread thinly.

'Infiltration.'

chapter one
hunter and hunted

Some weeks later ...

Cameron hunkered close to the ground, light drizzle spattering on his back. His night vision painted the world in green and black.

He held himself perfectly still, keeping his target firmly fixed in the illuminated square on his Head-Up Display. Slowly, with the patience of a true predator, Cameron brought his gun-arm up. The targeting reticule – a green diamond on his display – steadily converged on the square.

The target tensed. The first sign that they had been aware of any danger.

Cameron froze. His stealth abilities had come a long way. His daily training schedule was obviously paying off. Being a monster wasn't something he'd ever wanted to grow used to, but since he was stuck with it, he had to make the best of a bad situation. That meant learning to adapt – learning to move with more grace and skill, and less like the messed-up Frankenstein's monster he appeared to be. He'd never be an expert stalker, but he'd done well to get this close to such a nervous quarry . . .

The target's head suddenly snapped up, eyes scanning the night.

Cameron swore inwardly. He was sure he hadn't moved. Some sixth sense was obviously telling his prey that he was near. He would have to take his shot. Now or never.

On his HUD, the diamond locked inside the square. He thought, *Fire*.

And he fired.

Servos whined in his arm, countering the compressed-gas kickback from the launcher. The net unfurled as it sailed through the air, spreading over several square metres before it dropped to the ground, and Cameron's mechanical eye zoomed in on the target – just in time to catch a glimpse of the rabbit scooting away across the hillside and out of sight down a burrow.

Great. He had caught a roughly rectangular patch of grass.

Again.

Cameron sighed and stood up. In his arm, mechanisms turned and clicked like tumblers in a lock, and he knew a second canister had revolved into place, reloading the net-gun. The nets were fine and strong, but the gun could only hold a magazine of three. Even if he could squeeze three *hundred* nets into his arm, though, he wasn't sure it would have been any good. Although maybe if he carpeted the entire hillside with nets, he might stand a chance of catching something . . .

Cameron selected the 'Weapon Ready' option from the menu on his HUD and watched as the net-gun tucked itself away inside his machine arm. He wondered what the problem was. Maybe the targeting system needed some fine-tuning – the gun had originally been designed to fire bullets rather than nets, after all. The Monster Republic's technical whizz, Tinker, hadn't had any trouble modifying the weapon, but Cameron had never been able to master it. Deep down, he suspected that the problem was in his mind. He had fired that gun just once, and then only in self-defence, but even so, he had never wanted to use it again. Even in its new, harmless form, every time he used the weapon, his memory echoed with the shock of the recoil running up his arm, the smell of gun-smoke, the eyes of the Bloodhound filling with pain . . .

A low rumble caught his attention.

Engine noise.

Instantly Cameron ducked back down, his machine-powered muscles making the move at lightning speed. The sound was some distance off, but growing louder. Fast. Maybe that was what had spooked the rabbit. He notched up the gain on his enhanced hearing, the targeting square flitting about his HUD as it computed the trajectory of the noise, directing his eyes down the valley.

There! Lights rounded a slope in the middle distance. A vehicle winding its way along the narrow road that ran through the hills. An army jeep.

Ever since the military had arrived in Broad Harbour they had been running patrols across the countryside around the town. The routes changed regularly and at random. It looked as if the latest change was going to bring the soldiers right past Cameron's position.

It was too late to move very far, but Cameron knew he had to get out of the open. Keeping low, he scrambled behind a small, scrubby bush. It wasn't a moment too soon. A large searchlight mounted on the rear of the jeep burst into life, a stabbing finger of light feeling its way across the hillside. Cameron pressed himself down into the wet grass, his built-in light filter activating automatically as the searchlight swept over his hiding place. Dimming down the piercing light to more manageable levels, he zoomed in on the men in the jeep. There were six of them, all armed with automatic rifles, and Cameron didn't doubt they would use them if they spotted him. A moment ago, he had been the hunter. Now he was the prey.

But over the past weeks Cameron had been getting a feel for how the patrols worked. They might shine their searchlights everywhere, but they didn't really know what they were looking for. They were just probing the area in the hope of scaring something into the open. The soldier working the searchlight was the only one really paying attention to the landscape, watching for signs of movement. The others appeared to be chatting or even joking. They looked as if they were fully expecting to find nothing unusual out here, just like they had every other night. The Monster Republic would remain safe as long as the army stuck to their approach – and as long as Cameron and his fellow monsters kept their cool and kept their heads down.

As long as they stayed hidden, he reasoned ruefully. Like frightened rabbits.

At this thought, Cameron was filled with anger, colder and harder than all the metal that had transformed his body and changed his life for ever. Ruined his life, more like.

Once upon a time he'd had everything going for him: a loving family, solid grades, good mates and a gorgeous girlfriend. But that had all been taken away from him in one fell swoop. By Dr Lazarus Fry.

Fry's crimes were endless. He had planted a bomb at the local nuclear power station – deliberately timed to coincide with a school trip. Then he had picked through the rubble, taking the bodies and the *pieces* of bodies he wanted, before putting them back together according to his grotesque designs. It was all part of a secret plan to assemble a private army – an army that Cameron was supposed to have been a part of. Rebuilt using his classmates' scavenged body parts, he had been turned into a weapon designed to kill.

Cameron had escaped before Fry could put him to use, but the horror hadn't ended there. His mum and dad had rejected him – not even recognizing him as their own son – and when his best friend Darren dared to help him, Fry had punished Darren by burning his house down in a terrible fire that had claimed his mother's life. Then, to cap it all, Fry had planted another bomb at the memorial service for the victims of the power-plant blast, aiming to kill the Prime Minister and provoke an outrage, so that he could pose as the local saviour.

Well, he had provoked outrage all right. Cameron felt it every day. But his anger was mixed with guilt. Because he had once had the chance to finish Dr Fry off. To choke the life out of him and stop him from ever harming anyone again. But he hadn't been able to do it. He had let the butcher go.

That hurt, even now, but Cameron hadn't had any choice. Because even the bombs and the murders weren't the only crimes that man had committed. Fry had reserved a fate much worse than death for Cameron's girlfriend, Marie. He had somehow managed to transplant the brain of school bully Carl Monkton into her body, turning her into Carla – a psychopathic cyborg even stronger than Cameron was. In their final showdown at the memorial service, Cameron had been forced to use Fry's own bomb to destroy Carla – to destroy the body of the girl he loved. He had been ready to destroy Fry too, but the twisted doctor had claimed that he still had Marie's brain safely stored somewhere and could somehow bring her back. How could Cameron kill him after that? His only hope was that if ever Fry could be brought to justice, he might also be made to keep his word. It was a slender chance, but Cameron clung to the thought that he might one day have her back.

One thing was certain anyway: Dr Fry was the one who should be on the run and in hiding from the army. Instead, his creations – Cameron and the other members of the Republic – were the wanted terrorists. They were the monsters. The injustice burned in Cameron's veins like acid.

Gritting his teeth, he tried to shove these bitter thoughts to the back of his mind – imagining giving Fry himself a hefty shove at the same time. Down a very deep hole perhaps. The Monster Republic had access to plenty of those since they'd been forced to relocate their base to the abandoned mine beneath his feet. Their very own warren. Ideal for rabbits. It wasn't exactly Watership Down, but it was all they had for a home.

Cameron waited as the jeep passed along the road and faded from view, its lights searching other hillsides. As he went over to gather up his net, a message flashed up in his display: incoming call. He blinked on the acknowledge icon. A familiar voice came through on his internal communicator, slightly crackly with static due to the metres of rock between them, but sounding as curt and stressed as ever:

'Cameron, get down here. Emergency meeting.'

'On my way,' he answered.

Cameron smiled.

Not many rabbits had a fox on their side.

chapter two

hunger

Guard was jumpy.

As Cameron emerged from the tunnel that led down from the surface, the young monster leaped up from the bank of screens he'd been staring at.

'Rora's waiting,' he snapped.

'Thanks,' replied Cameron, eyeing him curiously.

Guard was normally too busy doing what he did best – what his name suggested – to give more than a nod to anyone passing through the iron gate that marked the divide between the old mine and the new base. Although with his vice-like steel jaw he looked uncomfortably

like a small version of one of Fry's Bloodhounds (minus the bloodthirsty attitude), Guard
was loyal and dedicated to his role, but he was
a monster of few words. Something was up.

The base was a maze of tunnels, dimly
illuminated by intermittent work lights, pipes
and electrical conduits running along the
walls. Several of the passages had been
concreted to form proper corridors, and the
monsters had converted various former
storage rooms into living quarters, a dining
hall, workshop and other areas to suit their
purposes. It was late, and most of them should
have been asleep, but the tunnels were full of
familiar faces. Cameron saw Owl, a wide-eyed
boy with radar domes like steel cups over his
ears, talking to Rehana, who would have been
the prettiest girl in the Republic if Dr Fry
hadn't given her scaly reptilian skin. They
gave Cameron a silent wave, their faces tense.
In fact, most of the other monsters he met as
he made his way to the control room looked
equally drawn. The Republic was a very
nervous nation right now.

It had a right to be, reflected Cameron. The members of the Monster Republic were all Rejects from Dr Fry's twisted programme of human experiments. Some, like Cameron and Guard, had been turned into cyborgs – a blend of human and machine. Others had had their DNA blended with animals', turning them into hybrids. There were even some monsters who were cyborgs *and* hybrids. But whatever their individual 'modifications', they all had one thing in common – they had escaped from Fry's laboratory or, like Cameron, been helped to escape. For years the Republic had lived a hidden existence, staying low and keeping out of the way of Dr Fry. Then things had changed. For a start, Cameron had arrived.

Cameron had persuaded the Rejects that they couldn't keep hiding for ever – that they had to fight back and stop Fry's murderous plot to kill the Prime Minister. Not everyone had agreed with him, but enough had. But although the Republic had thwarted Fry's plan, in order to do so, they'd had to come out into the open. The battle at the memorial service had made the national news. Soon, Broad Harbour was swarming with reporters, all looking for a trace of the 'terrorists'. In their wake came the army. All the Republic could do was dig in and try to weather the storm. No wonder people were anxious.

Still, Cameron couldn't help wondering what was so urgent that Rora would call him in early. There was no point trying to guess, though, he mused as he walked briskly into the control room. He was about to get the answer straight from the fox's mouth . . .

Rora was waiting for him, hands on hips, her pretty elfin features set in a serious, no-time-for-pleasantries expression. It might have been a trick of the light, but the fine russet hairs that coated the fox-girl's features appeared to be bristling.

'What kept you?' she demanded, gesturing at the two figures next to her. 'We've been waiting.'

Smarts and Slater. Chalk and cheese . . .

Small and slight, Smarts looked fidgety, like he'd had a few too many cups of coffee, but he still produced a smile – the first one Cameron had seen that night. His dark glasses concealed blind eyes, but Smarts sensed a lot without seeing, and often managed to remain more upbeat than most of the monsters, even in a crisis.

The contrast with the other boy couldn't have been stronger. Wearing his usual moody glower, and welcoming Cameron with a sneer, Slater paced back and forth on his powerful mechanical legs. The pair had never got on. After seeing Cameron in action, Slater seemed to have developed a healthy measure of respect for his physical abilities, but since Rora made Cameron equal second-in-command with him, Slater's resentment had grown. They would never be equals in Slater's eyes.

'I seem to recall using the word "emergency",' Rora added pointedly.

Cameron gave an apologetic shrug. 'Sorry. I came as fast as I could. The army have changed their patrol route again, so I had to take a bit of a detour.'

'Just as well their hunting skills are as

rubbish as yours,' Slater remarked derisively.

'I called a meeting, not a fight,' snapped Rora, turning her glare on Slater. 'So now's not the time to go starting one.'

At least she was spreading her foul mood around evenly.

'All right,' said Cameron calmly. 'So what's the problem?'

'Food,' said Slater, like he was talking to an idiot.

'Food? Why?' Cameron frowned. 'There's been plenty to go round.'

'That's just it,' replied Rora. 'We've been too relaxed about our eating habits. People have been taking snacks to their rooms, or out on patrol. Some have even been making themselves extra meals.'

'But why is that an emergency?' Cameron asked.

'I've run an inventory on the food supplies,' explained Rora tightly, 'and it's not looking good.'

'In fact,' cut in Slater, 'you might say it's looking bad. *Very* bad.'

Rora rolled her eyes. 'We moved before we were ready, Cameron. You remember what it was like.'

Cameron did – numerous rushed trips between the old safe house in the sewers of Broad Harbour and the new base in the mine; hurried installation of security devices; improvised electricity, light and heating systems. In short, a mad scramble.

Rora chewed her lip. 'The long and the short of it is, we didn't stockpile nearly enough food. We didn't think that would be a problem, but then the army came, and now we're holed up here.'

'We could have used some rabbit stew,' added Slater, with a significant look in the direction of Cameron's empty hands.

'It will take more than a few rabbits to meet our needs,' chipped in Smarts with a pained expression. 'The army patrols have made it incredibly difficult for our foraging expeditions. Too many of our food-gathering missions have had to return early to avoid getting caught.'

'So how bad is it?' asked Cameron.

'Bad,' replied Smarts. 'If we start rationing now, we have enough food for two, maybe three weeks.'

'So you see why this is an emergency now?' said Rora, fixing Cameron with a steely glare. 'At this rate, the army don't need to find the Republic. They're going to starve us out.'

A tense silence descended.

'So what are we going to do?' Cameron asked finally.

'We have to send out a foraging expedition,' said Rora. 'But something different this time. We need to target somewhere that can replenish our supplies overnight and give us a safety margin. A big score.'

'So, what,' said Slater, 'you want to rob the Food Bank of England?'

Cameron ignored the sarcasm. He had already figured out what target Rora had in mind.

'A supermarket.'

'Exactly.'

Cameron puffed out his cheeks. 'OK. Well, if Smarts can pull together some details on the layout and security system, we should be able to put a plan together in a couple of days.'

Rora was already shaking her head before he'd finished. 'Uh-uh.'

Slater stood bolt upright. 'Oh no, hang on a minute. You can't be serious.'

'So if not in a couple of days . . .' began Cameron. Then it dawned on him what Rora was thinking. 'Tonight? You want us to go *tonight*?'

Rora gave a no-nonsense nod. 'Can I take it that the "us" means you're volunteering?'

'Well, yeah. No question.' Cameron glanced at Slater, to make sure he was getting the willingness. 'But why so suddenly?'

'The supermarket I have in mind takes its big food delivery on the fifth of every month. In fact, they are probably unloading it right now. If we hit the place tonight, we can get everything we need.'

Cameron blinked his good eye. 'So if we're going to do this, it should be within the next couple of hours.'

Rora smiled. 'You read my mind.'

chapter three

night ride

It was an insane plan and it was going to get them all killed. Cameron had to wonder why on earth he had volunteered.

The three other monsters huddled under the tarpaulin with him must have been wondering the same as they rocked about in the back of the Republic's old flat-bed truck. But Cameron knew why really. Partly he still felt guilty about his continuing failure as a hunter – sure, a few rabbits wouldn't have made much difference to their food shortage, but they would at least have been a contribution. And if he was totally honest, he felt like he still had something to prove to Slater.

But it was more than that. Cameron was a member of the Republic and – regardless of what Slater thought – one of the more useful ones. He possessed dozens of abilities and enhancements, many he hadn't begun to master and probably a few he hadn't even discovered yet. Quite simply, he was the best monster for the job, and he owed it to the Republic to put his talents to good use. Sure, he was still the new boy and some of his fellow monsters didn't entirely trust him, but there were more who respected him and relied on him to step up and take the lead, a bit like when he was captain of the school footie team.

A small handful of those were looking back at him right now, sharing the bumpy truck ride as they headed for danger: Jace, Freddy and Tinker, sitting with him in their hiding place behind a stack of boxes on the truck's cargo bed. Rora had picked them for the mission, but Cameron didn't doubt for one minute that, had they been given the opportunity, they would have volunteered just like him.

Up in front, Robbie was driving. Cameron didn't know Robbie very well. He was another quiet one, like Guard. But unlike Guard, he easily passed for human. Although he had a completely metal torso, when he was dressed in a parka and a woolly sweater, he appeared to be an ordinary, solemn-faced young man with untidy brown hair. His sparse stubble also made him look older than his sixteen years. Old enough to drive a van without attracting too much suspicion anyway.

He was a good driver too, and soon the rough track from the mine gave way to the road, putting an end to the bumps and jolts. But although the ride had smoothed out, everyone knew this was where their journey really started to get dangerous.

'Do you think the army will be out tonight, Cam?' whispered Freddy.

Even with his enhanced hearing, Cameron had to strain to catch the words. The others were wearing quizzical expressions, like they hadn't heard a thing.

'No need to whisper,' Cameron said. 'If we can't hear you then nobody else can.'

He managed a smile, doing his best to appear more confident than he felt. His partners in crime looked like they could use a morale boost. 'We should be OK. At least for the first stretch. The closer to town we get, the more careful we'll have to be, that's all.'

'Yeah,' said Jace, with a grimace. 'There's *bound* to be patrols out.'

Freddy and Jace were twins and utterly inseparable. With their boar-like tusks and leathery-skinned bodies they looked terrifying, but they were actually really sound. They were wicked pranksters, though, always joking and fooling about. But neither was joking just now.

'We'll c-c-cross that bridge when we come t-t-to it,' Tinker assured everybody. He was small, with spiky blond hair and very geekish glasses, and his nervous stammer and the constant twitching of his face and limbs had nothing to do with the vibrations of the vehicle – they were a legacy of his time under Dr Fry's

27

'care'. Tinker was a brilliant engineer, inventor and repair man, but one thing he wasn't good at was oozing confidence.

Cameron wished he could boost morale some more – give the guys a stirring speech, like one of his pre-match pep talks before the team headed out onto the pitch. But this wasn't about a football game. This was about survival. And his own confidence was in short supply, Cameron realized as he reflected on how hastily this plan had been cobbled together.

Too hastily by far. He could still taste the desperation.

'The thing you have to remember, Tink,' Jace was saying, 'is that me and Freddy have done this a hundred times before. Well, not this exactly, but missions like it.'

'A hundred times,' agreed Freddy. 'You're not usually out in the field, but we are. We've been in some scrapes, but we always make it back to base, don't we? Like at Halloween, when we went walking around the streets in the open.'

'Oh yeah,' Jace joined in, laughing. 'And we

scared the heck out of all those kids – until we bumped into some with their parents: then we had to do a runner.'

'Rora went mental. Not because we nearly got ourselves caught but because all we came back with was sweets!'

Cameron chuckled. He should have known he could rely on Jace and Freddy to lift the mood. Their irrepressible spirits had overcome the air of tension. They also fired encouraging smiles in Cameron's direction. Maybe they had interpreted his silence as a case of nerves. If so, they weren't entirely wrong.

'So,' he said, trying to sound positive, 'are we all ready for a bit of shoplifting?'

'*We?*' Jace replied, grinning. 'You could probably lift a whole shop all by yourself.'

He and Freddy fell about in a giggling fit. Cameron didn't like to shatter their illusions – he wasn't *that* strong – but he and Tinker couldn't help but join in the laughter.

Suddenly the truck braked sharply.

Cameron cursed as he lost his balance.

'What's going on, Robbie?' he yelled.

'We've got trouble,' came the gruff reply.

As the truck screeched to a halt, Cameron shuffled over to the side and risked a peek out from under the tarpaulin. His night vision engaged, penetrating the rain and dark.

Metal barriers had been placed across the road ahead, and soldiers – maybe half a dozen, with rifles in hand – were stationed in front and to the sides. Two jeeps were parked up in a lay-by.

Cameron ducked quickly back under cover.

'Roadblock,' he told the others. 'Everyone down. And don't move a muscle.'

They obeyed without any fuss, pressing themselves flat on the cargo bed. Surrounded by the small fortress of boxes, they were pretty well hidden. But cardboard walls were flimsy and their hiding place wouldn't hold up under any close search.

'Absolute silence,' Cameron mouthed, his voice hardly audible. The others nodded. Jace and Freddy looked tense. Tinker's face was a frozen mask of panic.

As the truck came to a halt, Cameron turned up the gain on his audio sensors and listened. Along with the quick mental snapshot of what he had seen, sounds from outside were all he had to build a picture of what was going on. Robbie had left the engine ticking over, and that – plus the rain pattering on the cab roof – should cover any noise the monsters made. Luckily, Cameron's hearing systems weren't only sensitive, they had filters that meant he could home in on particular sounds, the same way a DJ's mixing deck could sample specific tracks off a record. So he notched down the bass rumble of the truck and the drumming of the rain, and focused exclusively on the booted footsteps approaching the truck.

They stopped by the cab door.

'Can you step out of the vehicle, sir.'

Robbie's voice came back: 'Do I have to? It's tipping down.'

It was a natural enough response. Robbie was famously emotionless, but Cameron couldn't help wondering if his nerves were up to this.

'Please,' insisted the soldier. It was not a request. 'Step out of the vehicle.'

The cab door opened and Cameron heard Robbie jump down.

'What's the problem?'

'Just a routine check. Nothing to be alarmed about.'

'I'm not alarmed. I mean . . .'

Cameron winced. Even to his ears, Robbie's voice sounded suspicious. What would the soldier make of him?

'Let me see your licence.'

There was a pause while Robbie dug around in his pockets for the document. He was either stalling for time or fumbling because of nerves. Cameron prayed it was the former. Impatient, the soldier decided to fill the interlude with more questions: 'Where are you headed? What's your load?'

'Just, uh . . .'

Please, Robbie, don't forget your lines. Cameron willed him to remember the cover story they had devised in case this sort of thing happened.

'Spuds for the local greengrocer's.'

'Late delivery, eh?'

'Yeah.'

Clomp, clomp, clomp, clomp.

A second set of footsteps stopped near the truck.

'Are we checking this one, sir?' Another voice, deeper than the first.

'Oh yeah. I think we'd better.'

'Is that really necessary?' asked Robbie, his voice squeaking nervously. 'It's only potatoes and I've got to be at the—'

'All you've got to do is wait right there while we search your vehicle. In fact, better yet, go and wait over there with my boys. Then you can be on your way. All right?'

Cameron's insides were knotted with tension. He could see the way this was going and he didn't like it one bit.

'Well, I . . .'

'Look, just do what you're told, OK? You've got your deliveries, we have our orders. Go ahead, check the back, Griffiths.'

'I'm on it,' said the deep voice.

Clomp, clomp, clomp.

Griffiths was moving along the side of the truck, heading for the rear. Cameron hunkered down tightly in the improvised hide.

Thud!

Tinker flinched as Griffiths swung himself up onto the cargo bed, his booted feet landing heavily on the metal. His footsteps beat a steady approach, filling Cameron's ears and drowning out even the pounding of his own heart.

Thud, thud, thud, thud.

Griffiths was closing in on their fortress of boxes. Cameron braced himself. Any moment now, the tarpaulin would be pulled back, revealing their hiding place. He fixed his gaze on the cardboard wall in front of him, expecting it to come smashing down.

They were about to be discovered.

chapter four

breaking and entering

A hand reached out, gripping the tarpaulin, ready to rip it away.

Scrolling quickly through the weapons menu on his HUD, Cameron charged his built-in Taser. Sparks crackled between the fingers of his mechanical hand. Anyone he touched now would be floored by a massive electric shock. It wasn't the greatest weapon against a squad of armed soldiers, but it was the best he had.

Suddenly a burst of static broke in on Cameron's enhanced hearing like thunder. Before he could turn down the volume, a radio crackled into life.

'All units, this is Control. We have contact in Sector Seven. Repeat, contact in Sector Seven. Target is a male, approximately two metres tall, moving fast towards the coast. Hell, he's moving like *lightning*. All units respond!'

The hand bunching the tarpaulin relaxed.

'Sector Seven? That's right next door!' shouted Griffiths. 'Just the other side of the hill.'

'Get down from there,' barked the officer who had first stopped the van. 'We're needed.'

'Suits me,' muttered Griffiths. 'Saves me having to sift through a lot of muddy spuds.'

Cameron heard the man turn and run to the rear of the truck. Then he jumped down from the cargo bed, while the officer at the front spoke to Robbie.

'All right, mate, get on your way. And shift it. We need to get going.'

Cameron listened to the sudden flurry of activity as the soldiers hurried to their vehicles; there was a scrape of metal – the road barriers being dragged clear. Robbie clambered up into the cab and the engine gave an eager rumble as the truck was set rolling on its way.

Jace, Freddy and Cameron traded relieved smiles. Tinker still looked positively terrified.

'W-w-what h-h-happened?' he stammered.

Cameron gave a wry smile. 'Male, about two metres tall and moving like lightning. Sound like anyone we know?'

Tinker's eyes widened. 'S-S-Slater?'

Cameron nodded. Trust Slater to cut it fine. But then it was a dangerous game, playing decoy. Cameron didn't have to like him any better, but he couldn't knock the guy. Once Rora had decided that the mission was going ahead, he had instantly offered himself up as a distraction for the patrols.

Get yourself noticed, Rora had said. *Just don't get yourself shot.*

Well, he had done the first part brilliantly. Cameron only hoped he was as successful at the second. He wasn't particularly worried, though. Slater's dog-like legs should help him run rings around the soldiers in these hills.

'Good luck,' he muttered under his breath as he scooted over to the side of the truck and peeked out through a tear in the tarpaulin. They were on the bypass now, coming into Broad Harbour. The last time Cameron had travelled this road he had been riding a skateboard, dodging and weaving between the traffic in a frantic getaway – a memory that made him all the more grateful for the less dramatic journey on this occasion. With the roadblock far behind them, it wasn't long before the truck rolled into the supermarket car park.

Cameron kept his head beneath the tarpaulin as he conducted his first scan of their objective. The place seemed deserted. The building and car park lay in darkness, but a few parking spaces were still occupied despite the lateness of the hour. Cameron frowned. Had the cars been left by customers looking for free parking, or were there still staff inside the super-market? Or worse, were the abandoned cars merely cover – somewhere for soldiers to wait unseen for the monsters to leave the safety of the truck . . . ?

Cameron gave himself a mental slap. He was letting his imagination run away with him. He could still feel the adrenaline from their close call at the roadblock zipping around his body, making him jittery. It was almost 2 a.m. – of course there were no staff inside. And the army had no idea of the monsters' plans, so why would they be lying in wait?

Still, Cameron searched the interior one more time for signs of life. But beyond the special-offer posters plastered all over the windows, he could see nothing.

'OK, let's move in,' he told Robbie.

Quietly cruising round to the back of the building, the truck turned and reversed into the supermarket's loading bay. Cameron tossed back the tarpaulin, led the others to the rear of the cargo bed and hopped onto the loading platform.

He stood to one side as Tinker scurried up to the alarm system junction box beside the garage-style door. Tinker didn't often venture out on 'field trips', simply because he was too valuable back at base, but this was where he came into his own – his 'tinkering' would get them inside more quickly and quietly than a brute-force attempt at breaking and entering.

Robbie dismounted from the cab and came over to join Cameron.

'I'm sorry,' he murmured. 'At the checkpoint. I didn't do a good job.'

'You did fine,' said Cameron.

It was only a half-lie, and there was no point in making Robbie feel bad. Under that sort of pressure, facing up to armed soldiers, anyone would have struggled. The important thing was, he hadn't cracked.

'And we're here, aren't we?' Cameron continued. 'We made it. Now we'll get this done and be on our way home in no time.'

Robbie nodded. He seemed stuck for words, but that was OK. There was nothing more to be said.

Tinker came running up, shutting his toolbox. 'All d-d-done,' he announced. There was a low hum as the door rolled up. Beyond lay a shadowy room. Tall square shapes loomed out of the darkness, like metallic sharks with black, gaping mouths. Tinker gulped.

'It's OK,' Cameron reassured him. 'They're just ovens. This is the bakery.'

Switching to night vision, Cameron swept the room quickly. It was packed with counters, racks of baking trays and largely empty shelves. There was probably plenty of bread-making flour here, but most of the supplies would be locked away in the cupboards. That wasn't what they had come for, anyway. They would find richer pickings in the store itself.

'All right,' said Cameron. 'Freddy and Jace – you're on shopping duty. Make it quick. Tinker and Robbie – stay with the truck and keep your eyes peeled out the back. I'll keep watch from the front.'

Robbie nodded. Jace saluted. Then, as Tinker and Robbie retired to the truck, Cameron followed Freddy and Jace inside.

'Trolley-dash!' called Freddy.

Jace grinned. 'Race you!'

Cameron opened his mouth to remind them it wasn't a game and that they should stick to the list Rora had put together. But it was too late. They were off and running through the plastic-curtained doorway that led out onto the shop floor. He shrugged and let them get on with it.

To them it was an adventure, even if to Cameron it felt like a crime. He reminded himself that the food crisis had left the Republic no choice. But that wasn't a defence that would ever stand up in court. Then again, if they were captured, their case would never get as far as court. He had no idea what the authorities would do if they arrested a bunch of monsters, but whatever it was, there would be no public outcry about *human* rights.

Time to shelve such thoughts. It didn't matter that he would never have done anything like this in normal life. This was just one more goodbye to that life. One more in a long list.

Quickly and quietly, Cameron made his way through the aisles to the front of the store. A little newspaper kiosk looked like a good spot for a guard post. It gave him a view out through the main entrance and across the forecourt. He could duck down behind the counter if he saw anyone walking by. It was unlikely at this hour, but it didn't hurt to play it safe.

All was silent outside, and inside, all Cameron could hear was the rattle and crash of items being dumped into metal trolleys as Freddy and Jace wheeled them up and down the aisles. The twins were quick – they must have made at least half a dozen runs back to load the truck already – but even so, Cameron wished they would hurry up. Guard duty was a strain on the nerves. Every time he heard the rush of a car on the bypass, his muscles tensed. Even this late at night, there were always people who had to go somewhere. Nobody turned into the supermarket though.

Cameron clenched and unclenched his mechanical hand. He drummed the fingers on the counter top, then stopped himself because it sounded too loud. The seconds ticked by on his HUD clock. He jumped at a crash from behind him, but then a burst of laughter echoed out. It had only been two trolleys colliding.

'Come on, you guys,' Cameron hissed loudly. 'Don't muck about.'

He went back to the serious business of watching. His gaze scanned along the rows of magazines that lined the shelves. Even if the colours were limited to varying shades of green, by upping the light intensification on his night vision he could pick out some of the images on the covers. Models, mostly. He saw one pretty blonde who immediately reminded him of his girlfriend, Marie. She could easily have been on one of those covers if she'd wanted. But she'd been bright too, smarter than models were supposed to be. She could have been a scientist. She could have been anything. Although Cameron sometimes hated what his life had become, he could never forget that Marie didn't even have that much.

He shook his head. Although he sometimes still missed her terribly, he knew he had to stop thinking about her. Fry had already used the memory of Marie against Cameron once, at the memorial service: he had told Cameron that he could restore her to life. For all Cameron knew, Fry had been lying through his teeth, but the idea had distracted him for long enough for Fry to get away. Now Cameron's thoughts of her were threatening his current mission. He had a job to do. This was no time for dreaming about the past.

Turning his gaze away from the pretty girls, he looked further along the shelf. Instantly his attention zeroed in on something else. The words BROAD HARBOUR above a picture of a person. He zoomed in, but it looked like the image was already pretty blurry, and he lost focus.

Curious, Cameron slid out from behind the counter, crossed to the shelf and picked up the magazine. His mouth dropped open and his eye widened.

The person on the cover was him.

chapter five

front-page news

The picture was a fuzzy middle-distance shot, and it was unlikely that anybody else would have recognized the figure. But Cameron could see that it was him right away. His face was mostly hidden by the hood of his parka, but you could still see the scars on his face, the glint from his mechanical eye, the hand that looked like it was wearing an ugly mechanical glove.

And he knew when and where it had been taken too – at the marina, right after he'd dealt with Carla at the memorial service. After the bomb.

His throat tight, Cameron scanned the headline:

BROAD HARBOUR 'MONSTERS': HUNTERS OR HUNTED?
That brought him up short. It didn't sound like the usual monster-related headlines – FIND THE FREAKS or PROTECT OUR KIDS FROM MONSTERS. Cameron flicked open the magazine and turned to the article. It was written by a journalist named Jack Austin. The name meant nothing to him, but the smaller headline took his breath away: *Are they really to blame or should the government be looking somewhere else?*

Was it possible that someone was on to the truth? He had to read the article properly. He spread the pages open on the kiosk counter.

Truth, they say, is the first casualty of war. When last month's memorial service in the town of Broad Harbour was desecrated by a bomb that exploded within metres of the Prime Minister, the authorities were quick to identify the terrorists responsible for the attack. Eye-witnesses who saw the perpetrators at the memorial service have described them as 'scarred', 'disfigured', 'freakish'. Blame was placed on a local

47

underground group known as the 'Monster Republic'. The army moved in. War was declared. The truth was forgotten.

I was there that day. I took the picture on the front of this magazine. Others were snapped quickly on cameras or mobile phones, but whatever their source, all the photographs have two things in common. First, they are, like the moments of panic that followed the explosion, chaotic and confused. And second, none of the pictures show any crime being committed. And yet the stories that have emerged in the aftermath of the bombing have all unquestioningly accepted the government line – the Monster Republic is to blame. Anyone questioning this version of events has been dismissed.

And yet, why would a group of bombers planning to murder hundreds of innocent people remain at the scene after planting their weapon? Why have the authorities produced no forensic evidence to link the Monster Republic with the attack? What is *the connection with local philanthropist Dr Lazarus Fry, whose scientists were on the scene even before the local police had arrived? If we are to uncover the truth of what really happened that day, these are just some of the questions we must ask. But one above all – who is the real monster behind the attack?*

Cameron closed the magazine, but the words of the article still spun in his head. The idea that anyone cared enough to write a story suggesting that the monsters might be innocent was almost too fantastic to believe. His mind raced with the possibilities. Perhaps here, at last, was a chance for them to tell their side of the story—

Suddenly a bright beam swept across his peripheral vision. Cameron spun round. Light flared in the glass doors of the main entrance. Without hesitating, he dived behind the kiosk counter. But the beam swept back, stabbing harshly through the doors, and he knew, with a horrible cold certainty, that he'd been seen.

Shouts erupted from outside, followed by the pounding of booted footsteps. Running. Cameron, his heart racing, popped his head up from behind the counter. It was risky, but he had to get some idea of what was going on. He took it all in immediately, like the click of a camera shutter.

Two jeeps, one searchlight still panning back and forth, the other fixing its blinding gaze on the entrance. Troops fanning out from the vehicles, rifles at the ready and advancing on the main doors.

'Damn!' Cameron exclaimed. How could he have been so *stupid*? He'd been so distracted by the discovery that not all regular people blamed the monsters for the bombing that he'd failed to notice the army patrol coming. Now it was too late. Cameron ducked back down behind the counter. He needed time to think.

He didn't get any.

A burst of gunfire punched through the main doors, shattering the glass.

They were coming in.

chapter six

a shot in the dark

'Jace! Freddy!' yelled Cameron. 'Time to get out of here!' They would have heard the shots, but he shouted the warning anyway. 'Leave the trolleys and go!'

Stuffing the magazine into his coat pocket, he got on his hands and knees and crawled to the end of the kiosk counter. He was up in the 'set' position, just like on sports day when the starter pistol was fired. Only this time he was being shot at for real. The thought froze him in place, forced him to hesitate.

It was a scary proposition, making a run for it when bullets were flying. Part of him just wanted to stay put. Maybe even put his hands up . . .

For now there were no more shots. But just as Cameron was beginning to wonder if it might be possible to talk himself out of this situation, something dark and shaped like a tin can flew in through the shattered doorway. It skittered across the floor and thunked into the far wall, hissing like an angry snake.

Cameron, low down, poked his head out for a look. White smoke was billowing out of the canister, spreading a cloud over the room. Immediately, warnings flashed on his HUD: a big blinking skull and crossbones. Toxic fumes! Cameron felt a rawness burning his throat, like acid going down. His one good eye was stinging like crazy. He started coughing. Frantically he cycled through the menu and called up what he needed.

BACKUP OXYGEN SYSTEM ACTIVATED.

Cameron breathed a sigh of relief. His emergency supply of oxygen had saved him from drowning once before when it started automatically. Apparently, Dr Fry hadn't installed an auto-trigger to respond to poisoned gas, but that didn't matter. Cameron could breathe again.

The air wouldn't last for ever though, and the soldiers were coming. He had to get moving. Hoping the smoke would cover his retreat, Cameron launched himself into a run for the nearest aisle.

More shots cracked out. Bullets zinged past him. He tried to dodge, but the cleaners had done too good a job of polishing the floor and he lost his footing on the slippery tiles. He stumbled to one side, careering into the nearest shelf and a pile of neatly stacked cereal boxes. The boxes went flying and Cameron crashed to the floor.

He could hear the soldiers tramping up now, double-timing it to the main doors, glass crunching under their boots as they stormed in. Their faces loomed through the smoke, deformed and misshapen, with bulging eyes and blunt, terrifying snouts. For a moment Cameron thought that it was Fry's monsters that had tracked them down, not soldiers at all. Then the cloud of tear gas thinned and he could see that the strange faces were gas masks.

The cloud had thinned . . . He was in plain sight!

'Hold it!' a soldier shouted, his voice muffled by his gas mask. 'Don't move!'

Cameron sprang to his feet, grabbed the top shelf and pulled, launching himself up and over. Legs braced, he landed perfectly and set off at a sprint along the next aisle, having put a shelf of cereal packets between him and the soldiers.

All the same, they opened fire.

Bullets punched through the boxes and raked the shelf opposite, spraying big messy clouds of flour and sugar after Cameron. Further along, jam jars and sauce bottles exploded, spattering their contents over the shelves and floor.

At the intersection with the central aisle that ran the length of the supermarket, he glanced left and right. He spotted Jace six aisles down, still wrestling with a trolley.

'Leave it!' Cameron yelled. 'Get back to the bakery! Get out!'

His hearing zeroed in on multiple sources of movement: soldiers charging up the aisles on either side, trying to outflank him. Before he'd even finished having the idea, Cameron lunged at the shelf to his right, pushing with his cybernetic arm. The servos whined loudly as he smashed the whole structure over. It crashed into the next shelf along, blocking the way for one group of soldiers as he turned and slammed against the right-hand shelf. He'd lost some momentum and it didn't break free, but the jolt spilled most of its contents over the aisle. The rolling cans and broken bottles might slow the other soldiers down, at least.

Scooping up some of the loose cans, Cameron ran on to the end of the aisle, nearly colliding with Freddy as the tusked monster hurtled round the corner.

'Where's Jace?' he demanded.

'Coming,' said Cameron, searching left. 'I think.'

A burst of gunfire. Bullets chewed at the

tiling close to Cameron's feet. He shoved Freddy aside with his shoulder. 'Get moving!'

Spinning, he saw two soldiers directly facing him at the end of the aisle. Their rifles were coming up, barrels aiming for his chest. His HUD zoomed in on them, highlighting and targeting each one. Cocking his arm, Cameron flung a pair of cans in a rapid one-two.

The cans sailed through the air in clean, swift arcs. One smacked the first soldier in the side of the head with enough force to dent his metal helmet. The other man ducked aside, but the can still clipped his left arm. The first reeled and fell. The second dropped to his knees and – ignoring the pain – raised his rifle to his shoulder and pulled the trigger.

Cameron threw himself left. Alarms pinged frantically in his head, warning him just how close the bullets had cut past him. He didn't need the alert – he had practically felt them. Off to the side, he could hear the other soldiers racing towards him. They'd obviously found a detour around the toppled shelf.

Time to go.

Breaking into a sprint, Cameron raced along the back wall. To his right, aisles flashed past. At first he caught the occasional glimpse of soldiers, but he quickly left them behind. At the far end of the store, Freddy was crouched by the door to the bakery. Beyond lay the truck – and freedom.

Cameron skidded to a halt. 'Let's get going!'

'Where's Jace?' shouted Freddy.

Cameron's face fell.

'I thought he was with you.'

Freddy shook his head. 'He hasn't come through here.'

Another burst of gunfire crackled through the store. Cameron could no longer hear the steps of the soldiers but they had to be moving up. Perhaps stealthily, perhaps in a hurry. They had to get out. Fast. Where the hell was Jace?

Right on cue, Jace reappeared round the end of a shelf about four aisles along. He looked terrified, but he was still tugging his trolley.

'Leave it, for God's sake!' Cameron cried, waving to him urgently. 'Come on!'

'But we need it!' yelled Jace.

'If we don't get out of here now, we're dead!' screamed Cameron.

For a moment Jace hesitated.

Two bursts of gunfire, short and sharp, rang out. Deafening in the confines of the store. The noise left Cameron's ears ringing, but he was sure he heard something after the shots.

A pained cry.

Still clutching the trolley, Jace slid to the floor.

'Jace!' Freddy took three quick steps towards his brother before Cameron caught his arm.

'Get to the truck,' he yelled. 'I'll help him.'

Without waiting to see if his order was being obeyed, Cameron dropped his head and raced forward. Rifles spat as he crossed between shelves. Bullets blew plaster from the wall. Throwing himself flat, he slid the last few metres on his belly, reaching out with his right arm to pull Jace into cover behind a big refrigerator unit.

Jace was clutching at his side, terror painted vividly all over his face. Cameron looked back towards the bakery and their escape route. The plastic curtain was still flapping from where Freddy had bolted through. There were only fifteen metres between them and the same doorway, but it might as well have been fifteen miles.

They were trapped.

They were trapped, and Jace was hurt. Cameron didn't know how badly.

Their only chance was to make a break for it. If he laid down enough covering fire, maybe they might make it. He reached up to the shelves above him for whatever ammunition they had to offer. Milk cartons. Not great, but they would have to do.

With that, Cameron leaped to his feet, going into a frenzy of grabbing and hurling items from the refrigerator. The plastic containers exploded down the aisle, showering the supermarket with milk. The soldiers answered the volley of cartons with live rounds, but Cameron was ducking and weaving too fast.

The hail of gunfire abated for a moment.

This was it. Gripping Jace around his shoulders, Cameron braced himself.

'Stay with me, Jace,' he snarled. 'Come on!'

Then he turned and launched them both towards the plastic curtain.

The power of Cameron's motor-enhanced legs propelled them both into the air. Bullets buzzed around them, but the soldiers couldn't have been expecting such a superhuman leap, and their aim was way off. With a plastic clatter, Cameron flew through the curtain, rolling as he hit the floor, doing his best to use his own body to protect Jace.

He glanced about. Ovens surrounded them. Steel-topped tables and rows of bread tins. They'd made it! Ahead of them, the loading bay was open and waiting. Freddy was framed in the doorway, waving an arm at them.

'Truck's fired up! Let's get going!'

Hugging Jace to him, Cameron charged at the edge of the platform and leaped onto the back of the truck. Freddy was beside him as he laid Jace down.

'Is he OK?' he demanded.

'He's hurt,' admitted Cameron.

'*What?* How badly?'

'I don't know.' Cameron banged on the back of the driver's cab. 'Get us out of here, Robbie!'

'Uh, Cameron,' said Freddy. 'I think we have another problem.'

Cameron followed the line of Freddy's pointing finger. From both sides of the car park, army jeeps were screeching in to block the exits.

There was no way out.

chapter seven

desperate times

Robbie gunned the engine and the truck leaped forward.

'Go left! Go left!' yelled Cameron. 'There has to be another exit.'

Soldiers were charging in on them from both sides. The *crack-crack* of gunfire followed them all the way across the car park. Bullets hammered into metal, or ricocheted off the sides of the vehicle. There was a violent lurch as the truck bumped over a flower bed.

But despite the din of engine and gunfire, all Cameron could hear was Jace moaning in agony. Freddy had him pinned down with an arm placed over him, but Cameron knew that every jolt of the truck would be rippling through his body, making his wounds worse.

Joining the shouts and shots, there was a screech of tyres and Tinker cried out from up front in the cab. Cameron, fighting to keep his balance as the truck swerved, popped his head up to see what was going on.

Robbie had steered them round into the forecourt of the supermarket petrol station, but army jeeps had blocked that exit too. Bullets were still pelting the sides and rear of the truck like a hailstorm of lead.

'We're t-t-trapped!' cried Tinker desperately. 'What do we do?'

'We have to break through,' shouted Cameron. 'It's the only way!'

Without waiting to hear any arguments, Robbie floored the accelerator.

The truck lurched again, hurtling forward. Cameron dropped down, pressing himself flat to the cargo bed. 'Hold on!' he yelled.

But his warning was drowned out by an almighty crash as the truck struck the bonnet of a jeep. The violent jolt shook right through them, but it sounded a lot worse for the other vehicle. As they sped past, Cameron saw the jeep rolling over from the force of the impact. With a sharp *crack* it burst into flames. They sped on.

More shots rang out, but the truck was out on the road now, the shouting soldiers dropping away in their wake. Hopefully – please, *please*, he begged – the soldiers would be too busy getting their comrades out of the stricken vehicle to come after them straight away.

Cameron lay still for a moment, sprawled on the cargo bed, just catching his breath and not really believing they had made it out alive. Then he became aware of a warm, wet puddle spreading under the palm of his human hand, and he knew without looking that it was Jace's blood.

'Clear a path! Get out the way!'

Cameron pushed through the rabble of monsters choking the corridor. Word of the disaster had spread like wildfire, and it seemed like every member of the Republic had been waiting for them, anxious for information or with offers of help. Now Cameron had another battle on his hands just to carry Jace through to Tinker's workshop. Monsters crowded in from all directions, jostling him dangerously.

'Look, just BACK OFF!' roared Cameron.

A shocked silence fell, but Cameron didn't feel guilty. He didn't have time for courtesies.

'Cameron!' Rora called, fighting her own way through the throng. 'What the hell happened?'

'Later,' said Cameron, pushing his way into Tinker's workshop and laying Jace out in the converted dentist's chair. He remembered his first time in that chair, when Tinker had poked around inside his arm to remove the tracking device put there by Dr Fry – how he'd shrunk away from Tinker's probing. But that was nowhere near as gruesome as the hole in Jace's side. He had bled all over Cameron's coat and there was more pouring out of him every second.

Tinker was hot on Cameron's heels, already hurrying round to the other side of the chair and operating the lever that tilted it back, levelling it out into a bed – or an operating table. Although his face was as jittery and twitchy as ever, his hands were steady as he leaned over the patient and conducted a swift examination.

Jace was completely out of it. He'd lost consciousness shortly after their escape from the supermarket. Robbie hadn't let up on the speed all the way home. If they had encountered another checkpoint, Cameron was sure Robbie would have just smashed through. Luckily they hadn't. The army seemed to have been so distracted by the events at the supermarket that the monsters had made it back without further incident.

Tinker glanced anxiously at the hordes of monsters pushing their way into the room.

'I'm g-g-going to need some sp-sp-space,' he appealed timidly to Cameron.

Cameron nodded, grateful for something to do. 'Everybody out!' he ordered. 'Right now!'

Nobody protested. The monsters withdrew until, as Tinker set to work, only six remained in the room. Besides Cameron, Tinker and his patient, there was Rora and Slater, of course. Lingering in the background, a fist held to his mouth, Freddy hovered in the doorway.

'Perhaps you'd better go too,' Rora advised him.

'I don't want to. I want—'

'I know what you *want*,' said Rora, her voice hard. 'But you can't help here. Go and help Robbie unload the truck.'

Freddy dithered, looking to Slater and then Cameron for support. 'Now,' said Rora, before anyone could come to Freddy's aid.

He bowed his head and Rora's expression softened. 'We'll come and find you as soon as there's any news,' she promised.

Freddy nodded and left.

'Cameron.' Rora waved him over, out of Tinker's way. Cameron looked over his shoulder to see how Tinker was doing. He had Jace's shirt cut open to expose the wound – a small, circular hole halfway up his side. Blood pooled on his stomach, dripping onto the floor. Cameron joined Rora, trying not to meet Slater's steely gaze.

'So,' said Rora, with forced calm. 'Tell me what happened.'

'It was going fine. We got through a checkpoint and went to the supermarket. We got nearly everything we needed. We were almost finished, and then soldiers came. I think it was just a routine patrol but . . .' Cameron swallowed. 'But I didn't see them coming. Until it was too late. The thing is, I'd picked up this magazine and—'

'You did *what*?' Slater burst out. 'You were *reading*?'

'Let him finish,' said Rora. Her voice was level but her eyes were as sharp as scalpels.

'It wasn't just anything, you idiot,' Cameron growled at Slater. His nerves were already at breaking point and he was feeling as bad as he could possibly feel, but with Slater on the offensive as usual, he was about ready to hit back. 'It was a story about us – the Republic. I had to check it out.'

He yanked the magazine out of his pocket. Some of Jace's blood had smeared the cover, but the headline was still legible:

BROAD HARBOUR 'MONSTERS': HUNTERS OR HUNTED?

'Read it for yourselves. Then you'll understand why I was distracted. It's not an excuse, it's just what happened, all right?'

'Right. And if Jace dies, that's "just what happened" too, is it?' snarled Slater.

Cameron bunched a fist, ready to punch him; but, using her fox-speed, Rora stepped in and threw up her arm to block the attack.

'None of that!' she seethed, grasping Cameron's wrist. 'I think Tinker already has his hands full with repair jobs, don't you?'

Cameron simmered, breathing heavily. He glowered at Slater, who sneered back, his expression like a dare.

'You dropped your guard,' Rora told Cameron. 'You let the side down and you let

Jace down. Keeping watch, that's what you were there for!'

Cameron lowered his gaze. The truth of her words bit into him. Rora lifted his chin, forcing him to look into her eyes. 'I know you feel bad about that. You'd better. And if you feel as bad as you look, then that's probably punishment enough.'

'Yeah, right,' scoffed Slater. 'He doesn't know Jace like we do. He—'

'Don't you dare!' yelled Cameron. 'He's my friend too!' He wrenched his arm free from Rora's grip and lunged at Slater. Slater's fists were up, ready for a full-on fight, but Rora was still wedged between them and he couldn't get past her.

'STOP IT – ALL OF YOU!'

Shrill and anxious and furious, the piercing voice came as such a shock it turned all their heads at once.

Tinker was glaring at them, red-faced and perfectly still.

'Stop it!' he repeated. 'Stop it right now!'

They stared at him. In the sudden quiet,

Tinker began to tremble. With an effort, he gestured at his patient. Jace wasn't moving. The monitor attached to his chest was emitting a single continuous beep.

'His heart's st-st-stopped,' Tinker informed them, tears welling behind his glasses. 'He's d-d-dead.'

chapter eight

flatline

Cameron stared in disbelief.

Tinker leaned over and planted his hands on Jace's chest. Desperately he started pumping down in a jerking rhythm. Cameron could see him muttering to himself, counting between compressions. He could also see that his efforts weren't doing any good.

'P-p-please,' Tinker begged. 'S-s-someone help me.'

Cameron didn't hesitate. He shoved the magazine into Slater's hand and rushed to the bedside, coaxing Tinker out of the way. Tinker's arms lacked the strength to apply the necessary pressure. Cameron's problem was just the opposite – he was too strong. If he wasn't careful, he could punch a hole clean through Jace's ribcage. The thought terrified him – and helped him focus.

Laying a palm flat on Jace's chest, he struck down on the back of his hand with his metallic fist. His left hand would act as a cushion, spreading the impact, while hopefully the punch would transmit the necessary shock to the heart to get it going again. Cameron counted to three, then hit again. And again. And again.

Nothing. Jace just lay there.

His eyes were open but empty. His mouth hung open, unmoving, in a blank expression of shock.

Shock!

That was the answer!

Jace needed an electric shock to jump-start his heart. In hospitals they had a special machine, but Cameron had something in his arm that might work almost as well – his Taser.

Calling up his menu system, he knew exactly

where to look. He heard the high-pitched whine as it charged up.

'What are you doing?' Rora had moved in behind him.

'Everyone stand clear!' he warned.

Then he withdrew his human hand and laid his mechanical one on Jace's bare skin. He looked at the command icon in his HUD.

Go.

Electricity crackled around his fingers. Jace's body convulsed in the chair.

Then lay still.

Cameron grimaced. 'Come on, Jace!'

He increased the charge and zapped the patient again. Jace's body gave another jolt as sparks shot up and down his frame. He dropped back down into the chair.

And gasped, like he was sucking in air after too long under water.

The monitor started beeping, sporadically at first, before finding a steady rhythm.

Everyone breathed a sigh of relief. Cameron stood back from the chair. There was still some charge left in his Taser, but he felt drained. Exhausted.

'You did it!' cheered Rora.

'B-b-brilliant!' managed Tinker. 'I-I-I wish I'd thought of that.'

He leaned in to examine Jace and studied the monitor intently. 'He's OK.' He nodded happily. 'F-f-for now.'

'For now?' queried Rora.

'Well, I've st-st-stopped the bleeding, but the b-b-bullet's still inside him,' Tinker explained. He gave a shaky little shrug, full of apology. 'I think I can k-keep him stable for a few days, but I'll n-n-need to operate to get it out. And for that we n-n-need proper s-surgical equipment. And b-blood.' He paused, his eyes firmly downcast. 'Food's not the only thing we're short of around here.'

Cameron sagged. The steady *beep-beep* of the machine and Jace's gasp had filled him with such a sense of relief and triumph. Now all he felt was defeated.

'Let us know what you need, Tink,' said

Rora. 'I have to go and speak to Freddy. Come on, you two.'

'Well done in there,' Slater commented as Cameron walked out into the corridor. The compliment was so uncharacteristic that Cameron glanced at him in surprise. Sure enough, he turned it into an attack. 'I expect that makes you feel a lot better.'

'Don't,' Cameron warned. He gestured back towards the workshop, where Tinker was again hovering over the unconscious Jace. 'No, it doesn't make me feel any better. I'm going to the hospital right now and I'm going to get everything Tinker needs for the operation. I can't do any more than that, can I?'

He turned to face Rora, who was just coming up beside Slater. 'But listen, we need to put that information to good use.'

'What information?' said Rora.

'In the magazine. The article.' Cameron tapped at the rolled-up magazine in Slater's hand. 'There's someone out there who sees our point of view. Or at least he's trying to see it. He knows there's more than one side to the story and he's trying to wake people up to the truth.'

'Rubbish,' said Slater. 'He's a normal, isn't he, this journalist? And all normals are anti-monster. They don't like us, Cameron. Or haven't you got the message yet?'

'They can't all be blind.'

Slater scoffed. 'If they were blind, we'd have fewer problems. It's the fact they can see that we have to worry about. Be grateful that photo is a blur. If they could see what you really look like, there'd be even more soldiers out there trying to hunt us down. That's what your precious journalist really wants.'

'No!' sighed Cameron. He was tired, and especially tired of knocking heads with Slater. 'If you read it you'd see that's not what his story is about. He says—'

'I don't care what he says! I don't know what his angle is, what game he's playing. What I *do* know is normal people not only don't care about us, they actually want us dealt with, disposed of – just like Fry does with all his Rejects. If those soldiers find us, it'll be game over.' He waved the magazine like he was ready to swat Cameron in the face. 'And your reporter's not going to save us.'

'Rora?' pleaded Cameron.

She studied him pensively, but said nothing.

'At least read the article while I'm gone,' he said. 'Will you do that much?'

Rora slowly reached out and took the magazine from Slater's hand. He seemed glad to be rid of it. She unrolled it and glanced over the cover. Something in the picture or the headline seemed to help her make up her mind.

'I feel like I'm in a hospital waiting room anyway,' she said. 'I might as well grab some reading material.'

'Thank you,' said Cameron. He gave her a smile.

She didn't answer with one. 'I'm making no promises. Just checking it out.'

'That's all I'm asking.'

'Well, you'd better get going, if you're going,' Slater told him. 'Good luck,' he added.

'Thanks,' answered Cameron grudgingly.

'It's not for you. It's for Jace.'

Cameron sighed. He should have known. He let it go. Slater was right about one thing. It was Jace who mattered, not their petty fights.

'Get Tinker to message me with the list of what he needs. I'll be back as soon as I can.'

Cameron turned and headed for the surface.

Back into danger.

He set off over the hill, an empty backpack hanging from his shoulders. Travelling on foot was far from ideal, particularly when Jace's life was on the line, but they couldn't take the chance of using a vehicle. The army were bound to have established more roadblocks since the disaster at the supermarket. They would simply have to trust that Tinker was right and Jace's condition could be kept stable for a couple of days – although Cameron hoped he would be back a great deal sooner than that. Alone, he could move fairly freely, and hopefully undetected, across the fields. Even avoiding the roads, he reckoned he could still make good progress.

The rain had eased off, but the night felt colder and lonelier now. Cameron trudged on, running for brief periods, then falling back into a hurried walk. He alternated like that for some time, staying low and exercising more patience whenever it came to crossing a road.

As he made his way towards the town, Cameron used the solitude to do some hard thinking. He imagined Rora reading the magazine article back at the base. She had to see it the way he'd seen it. She had to. And since she was leader, Slater would have to go along with whatever she decided.

Meanwhile, there couldn't be any harm in trying to find out a bit more about this journalist . . .

It was the sort of thing he could have asked Smarts to help with. But he didn't want to get Smarts involved. Not yet. Not until he was more certain. As soon as he could see he was nearing a built-up area, Cameron started using his HUD to search for an unsecured wi-fi connection. Once he was through and connected, he began searching for information on Jack Austin.

For Cameron, searching the Internet was just like browsing on a mobile, except that the screen was in his head. The search turned up articles and brief profiles, although none of them had a photo. The guy hadn't won any awards but he'd worked for several newspapers and magazines. He had a reputation as being unconventional and a bit of a conspiracy theorist, but he didn't come across as a weirdo. He seemed to be what he claimed to be – a journalist with an eye for the story behind the story. Had he really caught a glimpse of the truth about the monsters behind the lies?

Right now all this was only a hope. Hopes, in Cameron's experience, were pretty thin. But this one was worth holding on to, at least until he had investigated further. Jack Austin could be the Monster Republic's best chance of telling their own side of the story.

And in that was potentially more than just a hope – it might be their only chance of a future.

chapter nine
accident and emergency

Arriving at the hospital, Cameron hesitated outside for a moment as an ambulance tore into the Accident and Emergency department, siren blaring. Paramedics raced round to open the rear doors, revealing a man with an obviously broken leg who screamed in agony as he was stretchered inside.

Cameron tugged his hood forward to keep his artificial eye in shadow and made sure his sleeve hung down to cover his right hand, confident that this was one of the few places in the world where he wouldn't look completely out of place. Nobody would pay too much attention to one more accident victim wandering in off the streets – even if he did look like he'd survived a car crash and a nuclear meltdown combined.

He was just outside the main door when Smarts called him up on his built-in communicator.

'Hi, Cameron,' he said. 'Good news. I've figured out a way to manage the operation with Robbie's help.'

'Robbie?' said Cameron in surprise. 'I didn't know he had medical training.'

'He doesn't. But while he was at the lab, Doctor Fry replaced his heart and lungs with mechanical replacements. He's like a human life-support machine. We can hook Jace up to his system to keep him alive during the operation.'

Cameron grinned. 'Smarts, you're a genius.'

'It's simple, really,' said Smarts, sounding embarrassed by Cameron's praise. 'Anyway, all we really need now are some surgical supplies and the blood. Then Tinker can get started on the operation. We don't know

Jace's blood type, so it will have to be Type O Negative. It's a sort of one-type-fits-all blood.'

'Got it – O Negative,' Cameron repeated.

'If you go to the Major Trauma Centre, everything we need should be there. There'll be a special fridge for the blood. We need at least three pints. And some scalpels, bandages and surgical tongs.'

'I'm on it, Smarts. Just about to go inside.'

'Good luck.'

'Thanks. See you soon.' Cameron signed off, thinking once again how lucky the monsters were to have Smarts. His brilliant mind was behind most of the technology that kept the Republic safe. Now he might be about to become a life-saver too. If Cameron could provide him with what he needed . . .

Straightening his shoulders, he walked through the doors.

He found himself in a large, brightly lit waiting area. Rows of plastic seats were crowded with people boasting all manner of injuries. Two drunk young men had obviously been in a fight. One had a broken nose, the other seemed to be missing his two front teeth. In the far corner, a small girl whimp-ered and cried as her mother gently rocked her to and fro, as if trying to send her to sleep. Opposite the door stood a large desk marked RECEPTION. Beyond the desk stretched a wide corridor with beds down one side, curtains separating each one from its neighbour. In the nearest bed, a harried-looking doctor was trying to treat the man with the broken leg, who was still howling with pain.

The scene was chaotic to say the least. Cameron smiled. So much the better. While the doctor was busy tending to the injured man, this might be a chance to slip inside unnoticed. The receptionist sat with her head down, poring over some paperwork.

He strode on past the desk, hoping she wouldn't look up.

'Hello there,' a voice called after him.

She must have looked up.

Cameron stopped in his tracks, considering

his best move. He didn't want her getting too close a look at him. Clamping his good hand to the side of his head to cover his metallic face, he turned back to the desk.

'Sorry,' he said. 'Listen, I'm not really an emergency. Old injuries, that's all, but they're flaring up something rotten. I thought I might be able to get some painkillers.'

The woman frowned, but when she spoke, Cameron thought he could detect a trace of sympathy in her voice.

'We'll have to see what we can do, won't we?' she said. 'Take a seat over there and a doctor will be with you as soon as possible.'

'Thanks,' said Cameron. 'Do I have time to use the toilet first?'

'Oh, you've got time for that,' laughed the receptionist wearily. 'It's madness here tonight. I'm afraid there's a wait of at least two hours. It's just down the hall and on your left. You'll see a sign.'

'Thanks.'

'I'll need your details when you come back.'

'Sure.'

Cameron headed off through a set of double doors that swung noisily closed behind him. He hurried along the corridor, scanning the signs. His first priority was to find the Major Trauma Unit. After that, he could worry about breaking in and smuggling the stolen goods out – and doing all of it unseen. It was a tall order. But a friend's life was hanging in the balance.

The hospital's clean white corridors all looked the same, and Cameron was glad of the signs directing him towards the Major Trauma Unit. To his surprise, it turned out to be a relatively small collection of rooms, but its shelves were stacked with bandages, surgical instruments in sterile wrappers, and packets of disposable syringes. More importantly, there was a fridge.

With an electronic keypad on the door.

Cameron groaned. Tinker was so much better than he was at picking locks. But he didn't want to attract attention by breaking the fridge open unless he absolutely had to.

Kneeling quickly, he slipped back the thumb-
nail of his mechanical hand and tugged out the
thin cable beneath. Plugging it into the keypad,
he cued up a programme on his HUD and
thought, *Run*.

To Cameron's immense relief, the lock
opened quite easily once he had interfaced
with the system. Inside, he found bags and
bags of blood. He quickly checked the
labels . . . O Negative.

Bingo.

Opening his rucksack, Cameron carefully
placed five bags of the dark liquid inside. He
glanced around to make sure there was still
no one in sight, but the place still seemed
deserted. He said a silent thank you that there
hadn't been a major accident anywhere in
Broad Harbour tonight. If the Major Trauma
Unit had been in use, he could never have got
anywhere near the fridge.

Standing up, he hastily stuffed his pockets
with the remaining items on his 'shopping list'
and a number of other potentially useful things
– half a dozen scalpels, a pair of surgical tongs,

a bandage mask for burns, gauze, several syringes and a bottle of antiseptic fluid.

Now for the getaway. Easing the door closed, Cameron set off along the corridor, buoyed by his progress. He had secured what Tinker needed, and more. It was all going to be all right—

'Hey, you there!'

The voice echoed down the corridor from behind him, freezing Cameron in his tracks.

'What are you doing?'

The man's voice was coming closer.

Gritting his teeth, Cameron called up the Taser on his HUD. He didn't want to use it – didn't want anyone else to get hurt – but if he had to fight his way out of here, he would. Jace needed him. Cameron wasn't about to let him down again.

'Are you lost?'

Lost! That was it. Maybe he could bluff his way out after all.

Quickly, delving into his pocket, Cameron pulled out the bandage mask. He slapped it onto his face, just as a hand took hold of his arm and gently turned him round.

The man was Asian, fairly tall, with a pleasant smile laced with concern. His name badge identified him as DR VERJEE.

'Hello, young man. What are you doing roaming around at this hour? I don't think you're supposed to be here.'

Cameron put on a dazed and confused act. 'I'm sorry, I'm not sure where I am. Think it must be the drugs they've got me on for these burns.'

'Really?' said the doctor, a suspicious tone creeping into his voice. He looked Cameron up and down. 'Or was someone trying to discharge themselves, hmm?'

Cameron figured it was best to play along with whatever assumptions the doctor made. 'You got me,' he said, and surrendered with a shrug.

Dr Verjee shook his head and tutted. 'Well, that won't do at all. I think those burns of yours are going to need a lot more care before you'll be going home. Come along.'

The doctor slipped his hand around Cameron's arm and began guiding him along.

'Where are we going?' asked Cameron.

'Back to the Burns Unit.' He checked his watch. 'I should really be in A and E, but I don't think you're in any state to find your own way. You really have managed to wander off course. It was lucky I found you.'

'Yeah,' conceded Cameron quietly. He offered no protest and allowed himself to be led along.

A few turns and a lengthy stretch along a well-lit passage and they were at the doors of the Burns Unit, where Cameron suspected he was going to be handed into the care of a nurse. That was the last thing he needed.

'You know what, doc,' he said. 'I'll be fine from here.'

'Hmm. And of course you promise you won't try to run off again?' The doctor made no attempt to cloak his scepticism.

'No, honestly, I won't. And if you have to be somewhere, I'd hate to think I kept another patient waiting. Besides,' said Cameron, gently extricating himself from the man's hold, 'I'd rather the duty nurse didn't know I tried to leave, know what I mean?'

The doctor chuckled. 'Oh, I know. We wouldn't want you to get on the wrong side of Nurse Keys.' He grasped the handle and pulled the door open. 'All right then. In you go.'

The doctor waved him on and Cameron ducked through the doors. The Burns Unit was dark, the only illumination coming from a lamp at the empty nurse's station. It looked like Nurse Keys was checking up on her sleeping patients. Dr Verjee could still see him through the glass, though, so he kept on walking and took the first turning to the right.

He stopped. Waited. Then peered back round the corner. Through the glass, he saw the doctor hurrying away. Thank goodness.

Cameron breathed a sigh of relief. That had been hard work. He was just about to go back out the way he had come when a large woman appeared from one of the darkened wards and walked back to the nurse's station. She hummed quietly to herself as she started sifting through some papers.

Before she could glance his way, Cameron ducked back out of sight into the doorway of a private room. As he waited for Nurse Keys to leave again, he glanced down at the small whiteboard to one side of the door. It held the name of the latest patient who had been given the room.

It was a name that stopped Cameron's heart.

Darren Harper.

chapter ten

blast from the past

Cameron hesitated, staring at the wooden door.

It was a paltry enough barrier. No obstacle for his machine-powered strength. But the truth was, it might as well have been made of titanium. There were other more powerful things keeping him from entering. He wanted to see his best friend, of course he did. But recent history made it a lot harder than it should have been.

After Cameron had escaped from Dr Fry's laboratory, and after he had tried – and failed – to make contact with his own family, he had turned to Darren. To his relief, his old friend had willingly agreed to meet him; hadn't recoiled in horror at the sight of his new face – a patchwork of metal and skin salvaged from his classmates. But when Fry's foot soldiers showed up, Cameron had realized that Darren's eagerness to see him had nothing to do with miracles – Darren was being blackmailed by Dr Fry, who had kidnapped his mum, threatening to harm her if Darren didn't agree to lead Cameron into the trap.

When it had come to the crunch, though, Darren couldn't go through with it. He'd tossed Cameron his skateboard as a means to a quick getaway. He had saved his life.

And for that, Fry had made good on his threats.

Cameron remembered the news report on the TV only a few days later. He recalled it vividly, almost as though he was watching it over again. A suspicious fire had claimed Darren's home – and his mum's life. Until now, Cameron hadn't been able to find out what had happened to his friend.

Now he knew – Darren had been hurt as well. Was he badly burned? Scarred? Darren had been brave enough to look Cameron in the face, so shouldn't he be strong enough to do the same? Cameron gnawed at his lip. It wasn't the prospect of seeing Darren's face that was deterring him. No, it was the fear of seeing the look in his eyes.

What would he find there? Friendship, still? Or maybe blame and hatred? It was all too easy to imagine. Cameron hated and blamed Dr Fry every day – for the loss of his family, his friends, Marie. Everything. Surely Cameron would be the last person Darren would want to see . . .

Swallowing hard and drawing a deep breath, Cameron grasped the handle. Braced for the worst – he opened the door and stepped inside.

The room was empty.

The bed was neatly made up, but there were no cards or grapes on the windowsill. In fact, no sign anyone had been in here recently at all.

Initial relief gave way to a new fear. *Oh God*, thought Cameron. *He's dead.*

No, that was too horrific to contemplate.

People also left hospital because they got better, he reminded himself. But which was it? He had to know. Getting a hold of his runaway emotions, Cameron decided to take a huge risk.

Clamping the bandage mask over his face again, he slipped out of the room and walked down the hall and up to the desk.

'Excuse me,' he said to the nurse, who was still flicking through her papers.

She looked up, startled, laying a hand on her chest.

'My goodness. I'm sorry – you gave me a shock!'

You should see me without the bandages, thought Cameron grimly.

'I'm sorry, didn't mean to frighten you. The thing is, I'm meant to be down in A and E, but I remembered a friend of mine was up here. So I thought I could pay him a visit while I was waiting for the doctor.'

It was a pretty thin cover story, but it was all he could think up on the spot. The nurse recovered her composure and managed a smile.

'Well, you can't visit anyone at this time of night – but who's your friend? I'll tell him you came by.'

'Darren Harper.' Cameron nodded down the corridor. 'I, ah, saw his name on the door, but he's not in there.'

'No, he was discharged a few days ago. He was well enough to go home.'

'Oh. OK. Thanks.'

Cameron was puzzled – Darren didn't *have* a home. He hid his confusion from the nurse though. 'Well, I'd better get back down to A and E. Thanks again.'

He turned and hastened to the exit, preoccupied with questions about Darren.

Who was looking after him? Darren didn't have any family other than his mum. He was a tough, independent sort – in the best way – but he was still only fourteen. The authorities wouldn't let him look after himself. Someone must have taken him into their care.

Cameron needed answers. He wanted to be sure Darren was OK. Watching out for any other wandering doctors, he searched along the corridor for an office. The door was locked, but a determined twist of his hand was enough to break in. He hurried over to the desk and fired up the computer terminal. Hooking directly into the system via a port beneath his fingernail, he called up the records for the Burns Unit. The data scrolled down both the monitor screen in front of him and on his HUD.

Geller . . . Greegan . . . Hallard . . . Harper!

The record flashed up in a new window, revealing the details of Darren's treatment during the month he had been a patient, and that he had left the hospital a couple of days earlier.

But it was the final detail in the file that took Cameron's breath away. He read it twice to make sure his display wasn't playing cruel tricks on him. But no.

Darren Harper had been discharged into the care of Dr Lazarus Fry.

chapter eleven

a friend in need

Cameron ran most of the way back to the base, doing his best to beat the sunrise. Dawn was fast approaching, and when you were a monster, darkness was one of your best allies.

As he ran, his mind was on Darren all the time. He couldn't escape the thought of his best friend waking up in the lab, just like he had done – with Dr Fry leaning over him, running tests, coldly assessing whether he would make the grade as one of his monstrous creations – and sending him off to be stored or disposed of, depending on the results. As if Fry hadn't done enough to Darren already, now he was surely going to do worse. Cameron hated to imagine what hideous modifications the doctor might inflict on him.

But the terrible truth was that Darren would be a prime subject. He had no family to come looking for him. And he had been injured and needed to be repaired. Just like Cameron. Just like Marie. Another victim of an 'accident' put back together by the man who had caused it. No – not put back together; ripped apart. Changed into something else – metal bolted onto his bones, or animal genes inserted into his DNA.

Cameron couldn't let that happen.

He was on the home stretch now. He raced towards the base, constantly on the lookout for patrols. At one point he heard the burr of a helicopter and squatted low, watching it fly over the next valley. But it was only a civilian helicopter, nothing to do with the army. Cameron got back to his feet and moved swiftly on.

Light was beginning to spread out across the landscape now, and in his mind an idea was forming as to how he might be able to help Darren *and* find out more about Marie at the same time. He needed to get into Fry's lab, that much was clear. Break Darren out, the same way Rora had rescued him.

Of course, Rora wouldn't approve. Too risky, she'd say. But like a lot of things, Cameron reckoned it depended on how he presented it . . .

* * *

'It's too risky,' said Rora.

Cameron had to stop himself smiling. His life might have been turned upside down lately, but he was starting to learn that some things were still reliably predictable.

Rora, Smarts and Slater were all gathered outside the workshop. Tinker was inside, handling the preparations for the operation. Jace lay unmoving, his breathing shallow and painful to hear. But now, as well as being connected to the monitors, he was hooked up to Robbie, who sat patiently in a chair by his side. Smarts had just finished explaining how all those cybernetic organs inside Robbie's titanium torso would keep Jace alive during the operation. Cameron hoped that the blind boy would be able to apply his inspirational genius to working out the details of his own rescue plan. First of all though, Cameron had to convince Rora.

'Listen,' he explained, 'I'm not talking about an all-out strike on Fry's lab. I'm talking about a stealth mission. Get in there without alerting the guards and find evidence of what Fry's been up to. He tested his subjects, didn't he? So he must have the results of those tests. Back in school they always used to tell us, "Show your working." Well, Fry's a scientist. He'll have notes keeping track of it all. Maybe on a computer.'

Smarts nodded. 'It would be a closed network. Nothing we could access from here.'

'Exactly. So we need to get inside and locate a terminal with access to the internal database.'

He had to stop himself from adding, 'Like I did at the hospital.' He'd been careful not to mention Darren or Marie. If Slater – or even Rora – got the impression this mission was personal for Cameron, they would rule it out in a heartbeat.

'Think about it, Rora,' Cameron pressed on, seeing in her eyes that she was at least weighing up the idea. 'Yes, it's a risk. But it's a risk every time we venture outside. And it won't be long before it's a risk just sitting here and doing nothing. Someone's bound to think of searching this place eventually. But if we can get proof that Fry is the villain and we are the victims, that changes *everything*. We can take it to the press – this journalist guy – and tell our side of the story.'

Rora breathed deeply before meeting Cameron's gaze.

'You're right. I can't argue with your logic. We can't just hide down here for ever. For one thing, we didn't get nearly enough food in that last haul.' She held up a hand. 'Don't get me wrong, I'm not blaming anyone. Just stating facts. And yeah, maybe they will find this base sooner or later. But we have surveillance to warn us when that happens, and that should buy us enough time for an evacuation.'

'But then what?' prompted Cameron, doing his best not to sound too confrontational. He wanted to win her over, not get her hackles up. 'Another rushed relocation? More rushed than the last? We won't have time to prepare and pack next time. We'll just have to run.'

'I know,' said Rora, her expression pained. 'I know all that. But we'd have to send our best people for this mission you're proposing. And I don't like the idea of doing that when the authorities are on the alert and – as we've seen – trigger-happy. There's a lot in what you're saying, Cameron. But I just don't know. I don't like it.'

Cameron sighed. If he couldn't convince Rora, he'd have no hope of persuading Slater. He glanced away, struggling to think of some other argument he could put forward, something that would clinch it before Slater squashed the idea once and for all.

Slater spoke.

'I say we do it.'

A slap in the face couldn't have stunned Cameron more. Even Rora looked as though she was wondering what had happened to him.

'Yeah, I know,' he said grudgingly. 'I've surprised myself too. But I don't have to like this guy to know when he's got the right idea.'

'Thanks,' said Cameron. 'I think.'

Rora studied Slater carefully. 'You really think we can get enough evidence to convince the authorities?'

'No,' said Slater flatly. 'I said he had the right idea, wanting to break into the base. But there's a better reason to do it – we can see if Fry's got any Rejects waiting for disposal. Recruit them. Swell the Republic's numbers a bit.'

'More mouths to feed, you mean?' Rora replied sarcastically.

'Maybe,' Slater conceded. 'But you said it yourself: the army could find us here any day. If we stay the way we are, we lose. The Republic needs to get bigger, stronger. We need to be ready to fight. And if we get to strike at Fry's operation at the same time, that suits me. I wouldn't mind a spot of payback.'

'None of us would mind that,' said Rora, her eyes flashing sternly as she raised a warning finger. 'But this can't be about revenge. If we do it, it has to be about the things we've discussed. Evidence – and possibly new recruits.'

Cameron nodded. Those terms suited him fine. Better than he'd hoped for, in fact. Slater's recruitment drive would be the perfect cover to rescue Darren. With luck, they might even get there before Fry could do anything to him. Cameron didn't want Darren to be a monster like he was – he wanted him out, free and living a normal life. As for Marie, well, even if he learned where Fry was storing her brain, he didn't know exactly what he could do. But he didn't need to think about that now. And Rora didn't need to know any of it. For now, Cameron had everything he wanted. He could see it in Rora's eyes already.

His mission had a green light.

chapter twelve

rescue mission

'He's r-r-ready to see you now,' said Tinker.

Cameron was waiting in the corridor outside the workshop. He'd been there ever since the news had come through that Jace's operation had been a success. Freddy had been in with his brother for a few minutes already. Now it looked like it was his turn.

Cameron swallowed nervously. He knew Jace wasn't usually the sort to go throwing blame around – he was just too good-hearted for that. But a nagging voice in his head still worried that Jace might never want to speak to him ever again. It was only guilt talking, but it wasn't easy to ignore. Clenching his fists, he walked in.

The smile on the patient's face was enough to tell him that he could put away the guilt.

'Hey, Cam,' Jace greeted him. He was propped up in Tinker's chair, looking weak and pale, but his eyes had regained some of their characteristic sparkle. 'Looks like I'm going to make it. They forgot I was a monster. They needed silver bullets or something.'

'That's werewolves,' said Cameron, smiling.

'Whatever. You know best.' He paused. 'And that's what I wanted to tell you. You *did* know best. You told me to leave that trolley. If I'd actually listened a bit sooner, I might not have got shot.'

'Now, wait—'

'No, hear me out,' Jace insisted, 'because I don't get to do serious very often. I just want to say, thanks for coming back for me.'

Cameron opened his mouth to point out that if he'd been paying more attention in the first place, they might all have been able to get out of the supermarket unhurt. But Jace got in first.

'It wasn't your fault, so don't try to tell me it was. And don't argue with the patient. It'll get me worked up and then I'll burst my stitches and you'll have Tinker to answer to!'

'All right then.' Cameron grinned, holding up his hands in mock surrender. 'No more argument from me. Just – get well, OK?'

'I'll do my best. I'm only sorry I won't be joining you on the raid.'

'Oh, you heard about that? Don't worry,' Cameron told him. 'This mission's going to be a breeze. Save your strength. We'll need you again when things get really tough.'

Jace laughed. 'Good luck, Cam.'

'See you soon.' With a nod to Freddy, beaming at his brother's side, Cameron left.

He hoped he had sounded relaxed to Jace, even though inside he was brimming with tension. In the last few days, the green light for the mission had turned a distinctly foxy shade of amber. Rora was insisting on an ultra-cautious approach, with lots of planning and preparation. Cameron knew it was the only sensible thing to do, but that did nothing to ease his frustration. Every day that passed was another day for Fry to do something to Darren, and Cameron was running on pure impatience.

As he turned into the corridor, Cameron almost bumped into Rora, on her way to visit the patient herself.

'Any news?' he asked.

'Smarts and Tinker are together right now,' she replied. 'They should have a plan by tomorrow night.'

'*Tomorrow night?* We're not breaking into Fort Knox, for God's sake!' snapped Cameron.

An uncomfortable silence fell. Cameron was suddenly aware that the eyes of several passing monsters were on him.

'I'm sorry,' he said, lowering his voice. 'But there's so much riding on this. I just want to get going.'

'I know,' Rora answered. 'Everyone does. But if we rush into it, that's when things go wrong.' She laid a hand gently on Cameron's human arm. 'Be patient.'

As Rora slipped past him and into the workshop, Cameron headed back to his room, cursing himself for letting his feelings get the better of him. Rora wasn't stupid. If he didn't keep a lid on his temper, she would figure out that he had more at stake in this plan than he had admitted. Added to that, he simply felt bad for shouting at her. She was doing her best to give Cameron's plan every possible chance of success. She deserved his best in return. It was only a couple of days, he told himself. Only a couple of days . . .

* * *

Moonlight shone down on the mission team as they slipped out of the old mine and began the long trek over the hills to Fry's laboratory. They avoided the higher ridges, where they would be more visible, and clouds drifting across the face of the moon lent them an occasional extra helping of shadow, but Cameron still felt vulnerable and conspicuous. Slater had suggested holding off for another night – tomorrow's forecast was for better cloud cover – but even Rora had opposed that.

All the planning was done. Another day sitting around waiting would have been too great a strain on nerves already stretched to breaking point.

It was finally time to go, and Cameron was grateful to be on the move.

As well as Cameron, the team consisted of Rora, Slater, Tinker and a fifth kid called Crawler. Crawler was a bit like Robbie in that he wasn't a great talker, but in all other respects he was unique. Slater had found him unconscious in the sewers near Fry's lab one night, two years earlier. He had somehow made it through the disposal system alive, although only just. Tinker had managed to nurse his body back to health, but even he couldn't heal his mind. The great gaps in his memory included most of his past life – even his own name. The other monsters had wanted to name him 'Spider'. But he had protested, pointing out that he only had six legs. *'Call me Crawler'*, he had said coldly, and nobody had argued.

Fry had replaced the boy's own arms and legs with spindly, flexible metal limbs, and attached another pair to his sides. His body was so thin he always looked starved, although Cameron had seen him eat as heartily as any of the monsters. Crawler scurried along beside the rest of them, silent apart from the faintest whir of the motors powering his limbs. Each of his six legs, silver in the moonlight, ended in a steel claw, flexible enough to serve as a hand as well as a foot, and he scuttled along like a giant insect. His eyes, which always looked disconcertingly big in his gaunt face, burned with an intense hatred, as though he could think of nothing but Dr Fry and all that he had done to him. He made almost every other monster in the Republic nervous. He even scared Cameron a little.

Rora kept a close eye on him, as if she was expecting Crawler to be trouble. But it wasn't as though she could send him back now. They needed him for the plan Smarts had devised.

When they were about a mile from their objective, Rora called a halt.

'OK, Cameron,' she said in a low voice. 'You know what to do. Scout out the perimeter and signal back with the all-clear. If there are too many guards or any sign of the Blood-hounds—'

'I know. We abort the mission.'

But Cameron already knew he wasn't going to do that. Whatever happened, he was breaking into the lab tonight.

With a nod to the others, he hurried off, low and fast, his all-important night vision engaged, and every one of his senses on full alert. As he drew nearer to his objective, he paused and glanced at the sky, timing his moves to coincide with the cloud cover.

Finally he crawled to the top of a shallow slope and stopped. He had never seen Fry's lab from the outside before. When he had been brought here the first time, he had been dead, or at least dying, and when he escaped, Rora had led him out through the sewers. Now the whole laboratory complex lay before him – a cluster of dark buildings surrounded by a high fence, studded with security cameras. The cameras panned slowly to and fro, but Cameron knew he was out of range, and Tinker had a jamming device to deal with them when they got up close. There was a large expanse of open ground to cross to reach the fence, but if they were quick and went one by one – like Smarts had planned – there was only a small chance of being spotted.

Zooming in, Cameron's eyes searched past the fence. He was looking down on the rear of the complex. Lights were on in only a few of the rooms, and apart from the random washes of moonlight, very little illumination was being shed on the closest part of the yard. That would be to the visitors' advantage. He couldn't see any guards or Bloodhounds. Maybe Fry relied heavily on the cameras. Cameron smiled grimly. The good doctor would pay for that over-confidence.

He was about to signal to the others to follow him in when something flickered at the corner of his vision and he looked left.

Perhaps two hundred metres along he saw a figure lurking at the base of the slope. Pressing himself flat to the ground, Cameron studied the shape. Was it a guard? And if so, what was he doing? Cameron glanced from side to side. If he was part of a patrol, the other members would be close by. But there was nobody else in sight.

He zoomed in on the figure. It was a man, dressed all in black. In his hands he held a small rectangular object with a long cylinder extending from its front. He was aiming it in the direction of the complex. Cameron frowned. Was it some sort of weapon?

Even as he had the thought, though, Cameron's supercharged hearing picked up a tell-tale click. A shutter. The man was 'armed' with a camera and was taking snapshots of Fry's lab. The cylinder on the front was a huge telephoto lens. Zooming in still closer, Cameron waited for his HUD to focus, and was rewarded with a good look at the man's face.

With a jolt, Cameron recognized him – perhaps because he had also been carrying a camera the last time Cameron had seen him. It was the photographer who had spoken to him at the memorial service after his battle with Carla. The one who had asked who he was.

At once, the fuzzy image from the cover of the magazine leaped to the front of his mind. Cameron had destroyed that photographer's camera, crumpled it in his fist like an old tin can. But maybe he had a spare. Maybe he took that shot of Cameron, and then started asking questions.

Maybe he was Jack Austin – the reporter who had written the article suggesting that there was more going on in Broad Harbour than met the eye . . .

It would make sense. Who else would be snooping around Dr Fry's base of operations in the dead of night? Excitement and hope surged inside Cameron. But then he grimaced. He was in the middle of a secret mission. It wasn't as though he could just walk up to the man and ask him. Come to think of it, even if he was Jack Austin, the man in black looked like he was on a secret mission of his own.

The temptation was almost too strong to resist, but Cameron forced himself to turn away. He could always get in touch with Austin later. For now, he had to find somewhere else to break through the fence.

Darren was waiting for him on the other side, and this was another occasion when Cameron really didn't want to stop to have his picture taken . . .

chapter thirteen

lion's den

Thunk!

The grappling hook flew through the night air and caught on the top of the fence first time. Pulling down, Cameron tested the line, which stretched back to where it was attached to the launcher, housed inside his mechanical arm. It was secure. Tinker's latest modification to the net gun worked a treat.

Cameron had led the other monsters to a spot over on the east side of the complex, far from the mysterious photographer. Tinker had jammed the cameras and now the team were ready to break in. Seizing the thin line in his good hand, Cameron hauled himself aloft.

Crawler made his own way up and over, hooking his wiry hands in the mesh and scaling the fence with ease. But while the multi-limbed monster might have been given incredible dexterity, he wasn't strong enough to help anyone else. That was Cameron's job. Near the top, he leaned back, reaching down first for Rora and then for Tinker, helping them clamber up. Finally Slater, with those powerful legs of his, sprang in an impressive standing high-jump, and landed perfectly on the other side.

They sprinted for the wall of the nearest building. Clinging to the shadows, they negotiated their way round to a door, marked on the plans as a fire exit. Tinker was already busy, waving a small black device about the size and shape of an iPhone across the door's surface. A low beep sounded.

'The alarm's d-d-disabled,' he stammered.

Cameron looked up towards the roof above their heads, where he could hear the hum of an air-conditioning unit. This was where Crawler came into his own. At Rora's signal, he dug his clawed hands into the concrete and scuttled, spider-like, straight up the wall, his six limbs propelling him in a scampering run all the way up to the roof, where he pulled himself over the edge and vanished from sight.

Rora bit her bottom lip. 'Now we wait.'

Cameron listened to the tell-tale metallic clanks as Crawler tore at the air-conditioning unit. Then, with a dull sigh, the whirring noise stopped and Cameron turned to peer in through the tiny glass window in the door. A moment later, an air vent in the ceiling popped out and fell to the floor. Cameron winced. The plastic clatter sounded deafening in the silence. He hoped Dr Fry hadn't given the lab's security team cybernetic ears too . . .

He watched as one of Crawler's long limbs curled down through the hole in the ceiling. Feeling its way across the floor, it quickly found the door – which, with a soft *click*, swung open.

Rora turned to the others.

'Come on.'

Slipping inside, they found themselves in a simple, unfurnished hallway, a dark, empty corridor stretching ahead. Cameron held the door for Crawler after he'd climbed down the wall. As he passed, Cameron noticed the bitterness in his eyes again – even more intense, if that was possible. It was only to be expected. The monsters were going into the lion's den, the place where they had been made – or remade. The building seemed to echo with the memories of the terrible things that had been done here. For an instant Cameron's mind flashed back through his own experiences: waking up on Dr Fry's operating table; racing to escape through these very corridors with Rora; being cornered by the ferocious Bloodhounds in the waste-disposal chamber; the horror of the moment when he had seen his new face for the first time . . . He suppressed a shiver.

One look was enough to tell Cameron that his companions were all enduring their own painful memories. Slater's face was twisted with rage. Tinker looked terrified. Even Rora's usually calm features were haunted. It didn't matter that the building was clean and clinical, like a hospital. For all of them, it felt more like an evil demon's lair.

To them, Dr Fry was the monster.

'Come on,' Rora urged in a whisper. 'Let's not hang about.'

She led the team along the passage and further into the complex. The darkened hallway soon gave way to lighted rooms and laboratories. Despite the late hour, the place was far from deserted. Scientists and technicians walked the corridors, going about their business. There weren't many on the night shift, but they still made it difficult for the intruders to creep around. Progress was frustratingly slow.

Cameron acted as navigator. He had the building floor plans saved to his computerized memory and displayed in a window in his HUD.

'Where to?' he whispered.

'The morgue first,' said Rora.

Cameron nodded. It was their name for the

room where she had first found him – a cold storage facility where they were most likely to find Rejects being held before disposal. Plus, it was right next to Fry's main laboratory, where they might uncover evidence of his latest projects.

Rora held up a hand and stopped them at the next corner: the *tap-tap-tap* of approaching footsteps. She frantically gestured towards the opposite side of the corridor and they all scooted across into a doorway, crouching low.

Just in time. A pair of technicians strolled past, one of them flipping through a chart on a clipboard while the other said something about improved reflexes. Rora watched them pass and growled under her breath.

'We're wasting time.'

Tinker slapped a hand against his chest. 'I think I had a h-h-heart attack.'

'Nearly there,' replied Cameron. 'Come on.'

Waiting a moment for the technicians to disappear, the monsters hurried across the intersecting corridor and through a large set of doors. Chill air wrapped around them at once. The room was in darkness, but Cameron didn't need his night vision to know that they'd made it.

They were in the morgue.

Familiar shapes surrounded him. Hard metal examination tables. Sheet-shrouded beds. Banks of medical machinery, dead and silent. But no sign of any of Fry's subjects, Rejects or otherwise. The five monsters were the only living things in the room.

'There's nothing here,' muttered Crawler. 'We've risked our necks breaking into this place and spent hours sneaking around, and for what?'

'Relax,' Slater told him. 'We haven't checked out the main labs or offices yet.'

Cameron bit his lip. He shared Crawler's frustration. But the fact was, he was right – it was taking them too long to move around. They just hadn't anticipated the lab being so busy at this time of night. They were running out of time. More than the fear of getting caught, he was beginning to dread the prospect of finding nothing – not Darren, not a clue as to where Marie's brain might be stored.

'*Shush!*' hissed Rora, finger to her lips. Her fine russet hairs were prickling.

In the silence, Cameron heard what must have had her spooked.

Voices.

He scanned their surroundings. There was a crack of light under the swing doors that led into the next room – where the voices were coming from. Rora and Slater crept along the wall to listen in. Cameron simply turned up his enhanced hearing.

As he notched up the volume, he stifled a gasp. Suddenly he was listening to Dr Fry's voice.

He was right next door.

'No,' Fry was saying. 'This latest subject is a complete failure. A waste of time and parts.'

'What shall we do, sir? Put it in cold storage?'

'No, don't bother. There's nothing worth salvaging here.' There was the light clatter of instruments being set down on a metal tray. 'Dispose of it.'

Footsteps.

Rora and Slater backed away from the door, fast.

'Hide!' Rora ordered.

The room bust into motion. Rora and Slater leaped under one of the beds. Tinker shrank into the corner, cowering behind a tall machine. Crawler scurried up the wall to hang upside down in the shadows. Cameron glanced around frantically. Bigger than the others, his cyborg body was harder to hide. There was nowhere to go. Unless . . .

Crossing the room in a single bound, he pressed himself to the wall next to the swing doors.

Please open this way, he prayed.

The doors opened.

Cameron breathed a sigh of relief as they swung towards him, hiding him from view. He flinched as the rattle of trolley wheels clattered across the tiled floor, dangerously close. Two technicians came through the doors, pushing a familiar-looking metal table. Light spilled into the morgue from behind them, sending shadows dancing across the white sheet that covered Dr Fry's latest unfortunate Reject. Beneath the crisp linen, a human shape stirred feebly. From the laboratory came the sound of running water. Fry washing his hands of his dirty deeds, no doubt. Crossing to the door, the technicians wheeled the table out of the room, turning left into the corridor.

A moment later, Cameron heard what had to be Fry's footsteps, his soles tapping a purposeful rhythm as he strode into the morgue, preceded by his tall, thin shadow. He passed by Cameron, close enough to touch – the man who had ruined his life. His fingers itched to close around the scrawny neck again, and squeeze until Fry told him everything he wanted to know about Marie. He took a half-step forward . . .

From under the bed that served as her hiding place, he saw Rora's eyes widen warningly. Cameron stopped. He could read the message clear enough. Confronting Fry here would be suicide. Worse than suicide – it would get them *all* killed.

The moment was gone anyway. Fry passed out into the corridor, turning to head in the opposite direction to the trolley.

Cameron realized he'd been holding his breath, and let it out in a rush. The monsters emerged from their hiding places. Slater opened the door a crack to peer out.

'Come on,' said Cameron. 'Let's get after him. Maybe he'll lead us to a computer – somewhere we can get information.'

'No, wait,' Slater replied. 'What about the Reject? We can't leave them.'

'I say we go after Fry,' Crawler chipped in, his voice icy while his eyes practically burned.

Rora shook her head. 'No. Slater's right. As much as I'd like to nab Fry, we wouldn't stand a chance of getting him out of here. And besides,' she added with a meaningful look at Crawler, 'we're not here for revenge. Not this time.'

Cameron nodded, guilt gnawing at him.

Dispose of it.

In his eagerness for information, he'd forgotten that, coming from Dr Fry, those three cold words were a death sentence.

'Come on,' he said. 'Let's go and save that Reject.'

Checking that the coast was clear, the monsters slipped out. The technicians were already turning into a new corridor. Cameron led the pursuit, always careful to stay a safe distance behind them. He was expecting them to wheel their cargo into a lift and take him or her – unlike Fry, he refused to think of the Reject as an 'it' – down to the basement, where Cameron had nearly met his own end in the jaws of the rubbish crusher. But instead they turned off into a room on the same floor, large and dimly lit. Inside, the two technicians brought their trolley to a stop alongside a conveyor belt. One of them went to a control panel and stabbed a button, while the other heaved the body off the trolley and onto the belt with a thump.

Anger flashed behind Cameron's eyes. The

man might as well have been handling a sack of rubbish.

Cameron signalled his friends, and one by one they slipped inside. They watched as a steel door slid up in the wall at the end of the conveyor belt. Heat blasted out over the chamber.

A furnace.

They were about to burn the Reject alive.

The conveyor belt juddered into action.

'Hey,' said one of the men. 'Grab that sheet, will you? Doctor Fry said he doesn't want us wasting good linen.'

The other guy shrugged, reached over and snatched the sheet from the body as it started on its journey towards the fire. The Reject's head lolled to one side, eyes closed.

Cameron's heart froze. The young Reject's face was red and raw, scarred with bubbling blisters. But that wasn't what gave Cameron the sick feeling in his stomach. It was the fact that – despite the burns – he recognized the boy in an instant.

It was Darren.

chapter fourteen

discovered

Cameron didn't stop to think. He charged at the nearest technician.

Even at full tilt, he had enough ground to cover that both men had time to turn round. Their eyes went wide, and Cameron's target opened his mouth to shout just as he rammed into him. The man was knocked backwards, slamming against the wall.

He clutched at his chest, winded for the moment, so Cameron spun to deal with the other guy. He was backing up and grabbing for something dangling from a string around his neck. A panic button!

Cameron lunged for the device, but the man

snatched it out of his reach, putting his thumb to the button.

Before he could press it, six spindly metallic limbs flashed around from behind him, sinking sharp claws into his body. Bloodstains blossomed where the claws pierced his white uniform. The man's mouth dropped open, the panic button falling from his hand. Crawler's face loomed over his shoulder, thin features set in a vicious expression as he slapped an arm over the technician's mouth, stifling his scream of agony.

Cameron turned back to the conveyor. Darren's unconscious body was already halfway to the furnace, moving closer every second. But the first technician had recovered and was reaching for his own panic button. Before Cameron could move, Slater rushed past in a blur. He unleashed a devastating left hook that sent the man reeling. He hit the wall for a second time, and crumpled in a heap on the floor. At the same moment Crawler withdrew his limbs, letting his victim flop forward. He hit the ground with a heavy thud that made Cameron wince. The man was still breathing, but only just.

'Cameron! Help!'

Rora and Tinker were already at Darren's side, struggling to haul him off the still-moving conveyor belt. But he was too heavy, and the conveyor was threatening to pull all of them into the flames. Cameron joined them in a flash. Cradling Darren in his arms, he lifted him clear.

Slater raced over to the control panel and hit the off button, powering down the conveyor and shutting the roaring furnace away behind its steel door.

In the sudden quiet, Cameron looked his friend over. His right arm was in a plaster cast – a legacy of Darren's last run-in with Carla, when Fry's psychotic henchman had broken it to prevent him from helping Cameron. Apart from that and the burns, he seemed relatively unscathed, compared to other Rejects. Even so, Fry's tampering had left its marks in the form of a metal plate implanted behind each ear. Once he'd been given time to mend, with a well-chosen hat and longer hair, maybe Darren could still pass for a normal human. Whether he could ever return to something approaching a normal life was another matter . . .

'Well,' remarked Tinker, 'at least w-we achieved s-s-something. We've rescued a Reject.'

'Yes, I suppose,' said Rora, with a wary eye on Crawler. The gaunt insect-boy had acted quickly and saved the day, but it seemed Cameron wasn't the only one who had been left unsettled by the ferocity of his attack. Crawler, for his part, was staring down at his victim with undisguised hatred. It gave Cameron the chills. Only Slater didn't seem too bothered.

'Anyway, we should get out of here now,' Rora decided.

Cameron grimaced. He hadn't managed to find any information about Marie, but he did have Darren. Was it greedy to want *everything* that he had come for? Was it asking too much? Maybe.

He could see Rora reading the pained hesitation on his face. He wondered how she would react if she found out that he knew this Reject. Now certainly wasn't the time to mention it.

'Look, I know we don't have any data,' she said. 'No evidence. And I wanted that as much as you. But we can't hang around. How long before these two are missed?'

'I-I-I agree,' offered Tinker.

Slater shrugged. He glanced over at Darren, lying limp in Cameron's arms. 'Doesn't seem like much for all the effort ... but yeah, it's too risky to stay.'

'All right,' conceded Cameron reluctantly. He closed his human eye briefly and sent a silent apology to Marie. *I'll come back for you*, he promised her in his thoughts. 'Let's go then.'

'You're not ... going ... anywhere,' gasped a voice.

With a tremendous effort, the man sprawled in front of Crawler turned himself over onto his back. Crawler raised a claw, set to stab down. But the man's eyes rolled upwards and he lay perfectly still. His right hand lay on his chest, closed around the panic button.

Alarms blared out all over the building.

They had no choice now. They had to run.

In a frantic panic, ducking round corners and darting along corridors, the monsters raced back to the fire exit. Even carrying Darren, Cameron could still keep pace with the others. There was no sign of any more technicians, but he knew that luck wouldn't last. Dr Fry didn't take kindly to intruders – and he had more than alarms protecting his laboratory . . .

Out in the yard, floodlights poured illumination down on the complex and spotlights swept across the ground just beyond the fence. Cameron swore. They were going to be seen, no matter what they did. There was no better option than to make a dash for it.

'Go!' Rora yelled the order, and they all went at once, sprinting out from the cover of the building into the light.

Rora was fastest, skidding to a stop just before the fence. Crawler scampered past her and started climbing. Slater opted for a running jump and vaulted clean over. Slinging Darren over his shoulder, Cameron raced to catch up. He half expected to hear gunshots. So far, though, there was nothing but the alarms, not even the baying of the Blood-hounds. Just as well, because a wheezing Tinker was bringing up the rear, and Cameron had just realized that there was going to be a problem . . .

'I can't help you and Tinker over the fence while I'm holding Darr— this guy.'

Rora grimaced. 'We can climb.'

'Maybe you can, but not Tink.'

Cameron racked his brain for alternatives. There was the main gate, but that would be manned by guards – guards who would now be ready for them. He could count himself lucky that Rora hadn't seemed to pick up on his near-mention of Darren's name, but they were going to need a lot more luck than that to get out of here.

Rora's sharp eyes latched onto something and she pointed along the fence. 'There!'

Cameron followed her finger. Fifty metres

away, he could see a point where the mesh bent inwards at the base, like a ragged wire curtain.

A hole.

Rora led the way, Tinker and Cameron – with Darren still hanging over his shoulder – following. Outside the fence, Slater and Crawler paralleled their progress.

'You two get going,' Rora told them.

'You're kidding, right?' Slater laughed. 'I'm not leaving you guys behind.'

'Listen, you get points for loyalty,' Rora snapped, 'but there's no sense in risking all of us getting caught. Get going, both of you! We'll catch you up.'

Slater shook his head. 'Crawler! You heard what Rora said. Let's go!'

Crawler nodded and scurried away. Slater faced Rora through the wire for a moment, then he too turned, disappearing into the darkness.

Rora eyed the hole. 'Is this going to be big enough?'

Cameron quickly ran the computation on his HUD.

'Not quite.' He wondered why he hadn't noticed the hole on his way in, but then he realized it was some distance from the point at which they had entered. In fact, it was a lot nearer to where he had seen that photographer. Had he made his way into the complex too while they had been sneaking around?

Cameron glanced about, wondering where he was now. There was no sign of him.

'This is a professional job,' said Tinker, his clear admiration even managing to smooth out his stammer. 'Cleanly cut. And look, they've laid a connecting wire here to avoid b-b-breaking the circuit. Whoever did this slipped in without tripping the alarms.'

'I don't think we need to worry about that now, do you?' retorted Cameron. 'So let's see if we can widen this hole . . .'

Laying Darren down carefully, he grabbed one side of the hole in each hand. With a sharp tug, he wrenched the mesh apart, doubling the size of the hole.

Cameron ushered Tinker ahead. Then Rora slipped gracefully through without even touching the sides. Cameron manoeuvred Darren into place, so that Rora and Tinker could reach back and drag him out.

A shrill, terrifying screech pierced the air. Followed by another. And another.

Louder than the alarms, the sounds stabbed at Cameron's sensitive hearing like high-pitched drills. No – these sounds were more animal, more beast than machine. And they were coming from above.

Cameron looked up.

A pair of huge winged shadows soared over the floodlights. As he watched, another two flew out of a high window in the main lab building. The growing flock circled in the night sky like gigantic vultures. They were moving too fast for Cameron to get a clear view, but whatever they were, it was suddenly frighteningly clear why there had been no sign of the Bloodhounds.

Dr Fry had some new pets.

chapter fifteen

fight and flight

'GO!' yelled Cameron, pointing at Darren. 'Get him out of here!'

The winged creatures were still wheeling above the laboratory, but Cameron had a horrible feeling they were just picking out their targets on the ground. 'I'll draw them off!'

'You can't!' Rora protested.

'There's no time.' Cameron glanced up. The flying monsters were beginning to glide lower.

'There must be some other way!'

'There isn't,' he snapped. '*You* can't fight those things. I can. Now get going!'

Rora locked eyes with him, and he was surprised and touched by the concern in her gaze. Then he was up and running, his attention focused upwards, waving his arms to make himself a bigger target. Darting along the fence, he put as much distance as he could between himself and the others. He just hoped they were doing what he'd told them and moving fast in the other direction – he didn't have time to look back.

Announcing its attack with an ear-splitting screech, one of the creatures swooped – diving straight at Cameron.

As it streaked down into the light, he got his first proper look at the beast. Bird-like, with silvered wings spread wide, it was all the more horrific for being part human. Between the wings was a human torso, even thinner than Crawler's, and the face, similarly gaunt, had been reshaped into a grotesque mask, with the addition of penetrating eyes and a vicious hooked beak. Razor-sharp talons extended as it swept in, reaching to clutch at its prey. If Fry's canine creations were Bloodhounds, there was no doubt that the creature swooping down on Cameron now was a Blood*hawk*.

Cameron ducked as he ran, feeling the beat of the monster's wings as it swept over him, narrowly missing his head with its claws.

He watched the beast climb through the air, turning for a second attack. More screeches warned him that the others were making their dives behind him. If they all came at him at once, he would be finished.

Cameron charged on, dodging and weaving, and glancing up as he tried to keep an eye on all the Bloodhawks. It was impossible. He was going to have to start thinning out their numbers . . .

As the next one swooped at him, he lashed out with his right arm, hoping to catch it. But the talons ripped his coat sleeve and the creature flew past unharmed. Cameron grimaced at the gash. If that hadn't been his mechanical arm, he would have been bleeding profusely by now.

Behind him, a third Bloodhawk was making its descent. Ahead, the first had completed its turn and was coming at him from the front. Cameron locked onto each in his HUD. Then he raised his arm and fired, unleashing a net into the killer bird's flight path. The net spread open and the Bloodhawk flew straight into it, crashing to the ground in a tangled heap. It flapped about, shrieking insanely, but Cameron wasn't watching. He spun and loosed off a second net. The shot went high, the net sailing over the attacking monster. But as it unfurled, it dropped onto the creature from above, dragging it down to earth.

Cameron looked up as a fourth Bloodhawk, until now still hovering high in the air, called wildly and threw itself into a dive. But it wasn't aiming for him. It swept down to land beside its netted fellow, pecking and biting with its barbed beak and tearing with its claws. The one in the net added to the cacophony of shrieks. It was impossible to tell whether the other monster was feeding on it or trying to free it.

It didn't matter. Cameron wasn't staying around to find out.

He ran on for another few metres, past the first Bloodhawk, before he wondered what had happened to the one that had torn his sleeve. He searched the skies above, around, behind him, expecting it to swoop on him at any moment. But nothing showed in the HUD.

Then he spotted it – some way ahead of him, out beyond the fence, soaring high and fast.

Cameron's heart jumped to his throat.

It must have spotted the others.

He pushed himself on, faster. Charging straight at the fence, he aimed with his grapple gun and fired. As soon as it hooked on, he yanked it taut and pulled himself up the fence at a run. Throwing himself over, he landed heavily on the other side. With a deft flick, he unhooked the grapple and broke into a sprint, chasing after the Bloodhawk. So far it was still flying level, but that would change as soon as it had a good chance at some prey.

Cameron could hear the servos in his limbs whining as he pushed them harder. All he could think of was the Bloodhawk, clawing at

Rora or Tinker with those talons. His friends could never protect themselves, let alone Darren. The best they could do would be to abandon him and make a break for it. All their efforts would have been for nothing . . .

Cameron raced up the hill and crested the low ridge. There, on the other side, he saw the object of the creature's pursuit – a single running figure. Of the monsters, Slater was the closest match in height but it definitely wasn't him. Not unless he'd somehow acquired a black leather jacket. It was the mystery photographer. It had to be.

Just as Cameron realized this, the man stumbled and fell – a sign of weakness that was the signal the Bloodhawk needed. Its chilling shriek pierced the air as it lunged into a dive. The man hadn't finished picking himself up before the creature was upon him. He rolled onto his back, throwing up his arms for protection, but Cameron knew that wouldn't do him any good.

Cameron was closing in, but he wouldn't be there in time. The man was about to be torn to pieces. He glanced down at his arm. Even if he could hit with the net, that would only succeed in trapping the Bloodhawk and its prey together.

Inspiration struck like a slap in the face. It might not work, but anything was worth a try.

Still running, Cameron zoomed in with his HUD and locked the targeting reticule onto the creature: it was hovering over its victim as it scratched at him with its razor-sharp talons. The man on the ground was thrashing about, hitting out with both arms in a frantic effort to drive it away.

Cameron stopped, and raised his arm for a steady aim. He called up the grapple gun and primed the Taser.

He fired.

The grappling hook went shooting towards the Bloodhawk, the trailing line stretching taut behind it. Just as the hook dug into the creature's flank, Cameron discharged the Taser – sending the current along the line.

The monster flapped its wings in a frenzy,

letting loose a bloodcurdling scream. Tearing itself free of the hook, it launched itself aloft, leaving the man shaking in the grass. Cameron couldn't tell if the current had zapped him as well, or whether his trembling was down to fear. As the Bloodhawk flapped its way back towards the laboratory, he rushed over to find out.

The man had pushed himself up into a sitting position, wearing a dazed expression. He was fair-haired and blue-eyed, but his face was pale with shock. The sleeves of his leather jacket were in tatters, but apart from a couple of deep scratches to his forehead and cheek, there were no signs of serious injury.

'Thank you,' he said as Cameron approached. 'I can't thank you enou—'

He broke off as he caught sight of Cameron's face. No surprise there. With one quarter replaced with metal, and another quarter borrowed from his dead Nigerian friend Kwame, Cameron's face was never going to win beauty contests. But what *was* a surprise was the expression on the man's own face.

It wasn't fear, or even shock. It was *recognition*.

'I know you,' the man whispered. 'You were at the memorial service. You broke my camera.'

Cameron felt unexpectedly embarrassed. 'I'm sorry. Things were, um, a bit difficult at the time.'

The man gave a shaky smile. 'Well, I guess I can let it go, now that you've saved my life and everything.'

Cameron smiled back and the man shook his head. 'I can't believe it. You're one of *them*.'

'One of who?' Cameron bristled.

'One of the people everyone's looking for. What are the odds? Everyone's looking for you, and it's me who finds you.' He offered his hand. 'My name's Jack Austin.'

Cameron nodded. 'I read your article.'

'If you don't want to shake my hand, that's fine,' said Austin. 'But could you at least help me up?'

Cameron laughed. Taking Austin's hand, he pulled him to his feet.

'Wow, you're strong, aren't you?' said Austin, eyeing Cameron as he patted down the remnants of his leather coat. 'Oh boy, I'm going to have to sell a *lot* more articles to pay for a new jacket.'

In the distance, a piercing cry cut through the darkness.

'We need to move,' said Cameron. 'That thing may come back – with friends.'

Just saying the word made Cameron think of his own friends. They ought to have been safely away by now, but he wanted to make sure. But at the same time, he was burning to find out more from this journalist. Perhaps a few minutes couldn't hurt . . .

'Come with me.'

He broke into a run, heading for a small copse about a mile away. Austin fell into step beside him. He was young and fit – in his early twenties, Cameron guessed – and had no trouble keeping up, even after his recent ordeal. They reached the trees in little more than five minutes, and ducked beneath their concealing branches.

'So, what are you doing here?' asked Cameron as Austin caught his breath.

'Looking for answers.'

'Answers to what?'

'To what happened at that memorial service. To what the Monster Republic actually is. To what Lazarus Fry is really doing in that lab. Although' – Austin glanced nervously up to the sky – 'I think I may have found the answer to that one . . .'

Cameron snorted. 'Yeah.'

'I wasn't getting very far with more conventional enquiries – a lot of closed doors, and responses ranging from "No comment" to "I think you must be ever so slightly insane, Mr Austin".'

Cameron wasn't altogether surprised. 'So you came to spy on Fry's lab.'

'It was more surveillance than espionage.'

Cameron raised his one eyebrow. 'That's why you cut through the fence, then?'

'Ah, well,' said Austin, scratching his head awkwardly. 'I wasn't seeing anything from my vantage point, so I confess I slipped in through the fence. But I slipped out again double-quick when the alarms went off. I'm guessing that was down to you . . .'

'Yeah,' admitted Cameron. 'But that's definitely off the record.'

'Right. Don't worry. Everything's off the record for now. I would like to get something on record sooner or later, though. Preferably sooner. Whatever Fry is up to, he can't be allowed to continue.' He nodded back in the direction of the lab complex. 'I hate to think what else he might be cooking up. But it's the truth about the crimes he's already committed that I'm after. And that's *your* story.'

'Mine?' Cameron pointed at himself.

'Yours – and your friends',' said the reporter earnestly. 'Obviously we didn't get a chance to stop and chat at the memorial service, but my intuition tells me you're the victims in all this – whatever "this" is. I think the public should have the chance to hear what you have to say.'

Cameron drew a lengthy breath. It was tempting, so very tempting, to just let it all spill out of him there and then. Here was the first person – a 'normal', as Slater would call him – who was willing, even eager, to listen. But he couldn't stop and talk. Not out here. Not with Darren waiting for him back at the base.

'Listen,' he said seriously. 'You're right – we're not the villains here. I'd love to . . . tell you things. But not now. I need to get back to my friends.'

Austin nodded slowly.

'I understand. And I must admit, I was thinking more of conducting the interview over a cup of coffee or something, rather than squatting under a tree.' He grinned, dug inside the remains of his jacket and pressed a card into Cameron's hand. 'Call me when you're ready, OK?'

Cameron looked down at the card in his palm. He already knew what Rora – and certainly Slater – would think of the idea of talking to a journalist. But at the same time he felt sure that this was an opportunity he couldn't afford to let slip.

He closed his hand over the card.

'I'll think about it,' he said. 'See you around.'

With that, Cameron turned and jogged away. At the bottom of the low hill, he glanced over his shoulder, but Jack Austin had already disappeared.

* * *

Dr Lazarus Fry stood on the roof of his laboratory, staring out over the fence towards the deserted countryside beyond. Two steps behind him, Hardiman shifted from foot to foot, his eyes flicking nervously to the winged shape crouching at Fry's side.

'Report.'

'The intruders have escaped, sir,' said Hardiman. 'The Bloodhawks pursued, but Subject 501 seems to have, er . . . immobilized them.'

'Immobilized? How?'

Dr Fry raked his long, thin fingers across the feathered head of the Bloodhawk. Letting out a soft whistling noise, the monster turned to fix Hardiman with a fierce, questioning gaze.

'Well, sir, it seems to have used some sort of net-gun on two of them, and the third has a grapple-wound and electrical burns.' Hardiman cleared his throat awkwardly. 'I think Subject 501 must have learned how to use its Taser at range, sir.'

'Of course he has – he's a clever boy, Hardiman.' Behind his rimless glasses, Fry's eyes narrowed. 'But is he clever enough?'

'Sir?'

'There's a very old saying, Hardiman – if something looks too good to be true, it probably is. I wonder whether our Cameron is too young to have learned that lesson yet.' Dr Fry gave one of his rare, mirthless smiles. 'I rather suspect he is . . .'

chapter sixteen

revelation

'Cameron!'

Rora seemed almost on the point of hugging him as he trudged into the control room after his long and lonely run home. At the last minute, though, she held off, settling instead for giving him a firm pat on the arm.

'You made it,' she said with relief. 'Are you OK? I can't believe you just took off like that.'

Cameron nodded. 'I'm fine. How about you guys?'

She beamed. 'We're all back safely. Tinker's with the new boy now. Come on.'

Back in leader mode, she marched briskly down the corridor to the workshop. Tinker was just emerging from within and Slater was hovering nearby.

'He'll m-m-mend,' declared Tinker. He looked frazzled. His hair was dishevelled and his eyes bloodshot. The Republic had asked a lot of him these past few days – two dangerous missions, along with all the planning and preparation that these had involved, one major surgical operation, and now some intensive first aid on Darren. It was a huge burden to place on one small set of shoulders. Cameron hoped the poor guy would be able to get some rest now.

'Can we see him?' Slater asked.

At his shoulder, Rora clearly wanted to know the same thing.

'He's awake,' confirmed Tinker. 'So, y-y-yes. But don't go subj-j-jecting him to an interrogation just yet.'

'That's not exactly what we had in mind,' said Rora.

'Well, if you can tell us a few things first, maybe we can spare him some of our questions,' suggested Slater. 'Like, what can he do?'

'W-w-what are his c-c-capabilities, you mean?' Tinker removed his glasses and began polishing them on the bottom of his T-shirt. 'It's hard to say. I haven't c-c-completed a full assessment yet. But it looks like m-m-mostly m-m-minor electronic enhancements, m-m-mainly in the brain area.'

'You checked him for tracking devices?' quizzed Rora.

'Of c-c-course.' Tinker shook his head, as though surprised that Rora would even have to ask. 'He's c-clean.'

'Good. I guess Doctor Fry didn't get a chance to tamper with the poor guy too much before making up his mind he was no use.'

'But is he going to be any use to *us*?' said Slater under his breath.

Cameron shook his head at Slater's uncaring question. He had to remind himself that the only reason the sharp-faced monster had supported the mission was to find new recruits. Slater had probably been hoping for more monsters like himself or Cameron, or even Crawler. Fighters. If Darren wasn't going to be one of those, of course Slater wouldn't be interested. He didn't have an emotional attachment to the new patient and Cameron wasn't really in a position to complain about his insensitivity – not without revealing his own connection to Darren. Still, he couldn't let it go.

'Maybe he's like Smarts,' Cameron said sharply. 'With extra intelligence or something. We just have to find out more about what those enhancements do.'

'Let's go and talk to him anyway,' Rora said. 'At the very least we can welcome him to the Republic. Tinker, go and get some rest.'

'I w-w-will.' The boy nodded gratefully. 'I won't be f-f-far if you n-need me.' He withdrew down the passage towards the dining hall.

Suddenly Cameron spotted the flaw in his plan. When he had planned Darren's rescue, he had always imagined that their reunion would be in private. If he went in to see him with Rora and Slater in tow, there would be no way to hide the fact that they knew each other.

'What are you waiting for?' said Rora impatiently.

'Uh, maybe it would be better to leave it until the morning,' said Cameron.

'We won't keep him awake long,' Rora said. 'But he has a right to know where he is and what's happened to him.'

Cameron shrugged. 'You guys go ahead. We don't want to crowd him.'

'What's wrong with you, Cameron?' demanded Rora. 'You saved this guy's life tonight. Twice. He's going to want to meet you. Now come on.'

Seizing his elbow, she led him into the workshop.

This was it. Darren would recognize his friend and the truth would be out. Cameron's mind raced, plagued with the same worry that had stalled him outside Darren's room at the hospital: that his best friend would blame him for what had happened to his mum. Even so, Cameron hoped the real Darren was still intact. He would rather be blamed and hated than be met by an empty shell.

Steeling himself, he prepared for the worst.

Darren regarded them blearily from the old dentist's chair, like he had just woken from a deep sleep. He looked as if he was having some trouble holding his head upright, but he was sitting up in the chair and, despite the circumstances, Cameron couldn't deny that it was good to see him.

Darren blinked a few times as the group gathered in front of him. For a moment he stared at them blankly.

Then his face lit up.

'Cam! It's you!'

Cameron felt his face flush as Rora slowly turned her head to stare at him. Slater glanced from Cameron to Darren, incredulity in his eyes.

Cameron ignored them both.

'Hi, Darren. How do you feel?'

'About as good as you look,' replied Darren with a weak attempt at a grin. 'But hell, am I glad to see you. I can't believe it.'

'Actually, neither can we,' Rora remarked, her voice suspiciously bright. 'You see, we had no idea you knew Cameron. He neglected to mention it.'

'Eh?' said Darren, a portrait of confusion.

'I can explain,' offered Cameron.

'I think you'd better, pal,' snarled Slater.

Cameron couldn't help but reflect on how the roles had been reversed. They had all come in here to question the patient but now everyone was looking to *him* for answers.

'Darren's an old school friend,' he admitted sheepishly. He could feel himself flinching under Rora's glare. It had been easy enough to dupe Slater, but he felt bad for deceiving her. 'My best friend – from back in normal life.'

'Right, the one you ran off to see that time,' said Slater.

Cameron prayed he wouldn't mention the fire. He expected the subject to come up eventually, but he didn't want it dropped into the discussion like a bombshell right now.

'Yes, that one. But listen, I know I didn't tell you the full story—'

'You lied to us, yeah,' said Slater.

'All right, if you want to put it like that,' answered Cameron, his face burning now as Rora studied him wordlessly. He wished she would jump in and say something, even if it was to bawl him out. Somehow that would be better than her silent disapproval. 'But think about it. What actual difference would it have made? We all wanted to rescue Darren. I don't think any of us would have acted differently.'

'That depends . . .' said Rora slowly, her voice taut with anger, 'on when you realized your friend was in the lab. Was it when you saw him there, or before we planned the mission?' Cameron swallowed. He couldn't look Rora in the eye. 'Tell you what, I think it's better for everyone if you don't answer that right now.'

'OK,' said Cameron, surprised at just how much her restrained fury stung. Guilt assaulted him from all sides – guilt for his own deception, guilt for his part in Darren's fate, and guilt for what had happened to Darren's mum. What made it even worse was that Rora still didn't know the full story – that finding Marie had figured prominently in Cameron's motives too.

But if Rora was willing to let it lie for now, Slater certainly wasn't. He stared at Rora, and threw up his hands.

'What? He leads us all a merry dance on some mission to rescue his mate – a mission that might have got us all killed – and we're just meant to leave it at that?'

'What do you want me to do?' snarled Rora. 'Ground him? Kick him out of the Republic?' Some of the anger she had held back from Cameron now spilled out at Slater. Normally Cameron might have enjoyed seeing him get taken down a peg or two, but this time it just made him feel worse. 'I'm tired of all this bickering and in-fighting. We need Cameron! We need you, Slater! This Republic needs every member we have right now.'

Like a parent who'd suddenly remembered that a child was watching a row, Rora turned to Darren, who was looking on with an expression of total bewilderment. 'I'm sorry,' she apologized. 'This wasn't the welcome I had in mind for you. We're such a happy family normally.'

Cameron winced at the sarcasm in her voice.

Darren laughed nervously. 'It's all right. My mum and me used to fight all the time.' He lowered his eyes, and Cameron felt a knot in his stomach, certain that this was the moment when he would mention the fire. But then Darren simply smiled again. 'So – am I part of this Republic of yours now?'

Cameron blinked in surprise. He'd been expecting a stream of accusations. He was relieved that Darren didn't seem to blame him, but it was odd the way he seemed so calm. Maybe he was in shock, or denial – or both. Cameron wasn't sure whether he should be concerned or just relieved to be spared the blame.

'Well,' said Rora, getting a further rein on her temper, 'you get better first and then we'll let you decide that for yourself. It might not feel like it right now, but you're better off here than with Fry.'

Cameron bit his tongue. He knew he wasn't Rora's favourite person right now, but that only made him anxious to come clean about the other thing he had to tell her. Not about Marie – there was no sense in throwing that into the mix now – but about Austin.

'There's . . . something else you should know,' he ventured tentatively.

'More secrets you've been keeping?' said Slater sarcastically.

'No. This is something that happened outside the lab, after . . . well, after I fought those hawk things.' He felt awkward talking about that too, afraid it might sound too much like singing his own praises. 'You remember that article in the magazine? And that hole cut in the fence?'

'Yes . . .' said Rora slowly.

'Well, they were both the work of the same man.'

Cameron had their attention now at least. Briefly, he recounted the battle with the Bloodhawks and how it had led to his meeting with the reporter, Austin.

'I had to save the guy. I couldn't just leave him to get torn to shreds. And then, well, we ended up talking for a bit.'

Slater advanced, a hand out, ready to grab Cameron by the collar. 'What did you tell him?'

'Nothing!' Cameron growled, batting Slater's arm away. The boy seemed determined to make this more difficult than it needed to be. 'I haven't told him anything. But listen, we went to the lab to find evidence, didn't we? Proof of what Fry's up to. Well, maybe Darren here is that proof.'

'Nice way to justify your lies,' scoffed Slater.

'I'm listening,' said Rora, flashing a warning look at Slater.

'This Austin guy knows there's something suspicious going on with Fry. He's the only one who isn't gunning for us. But he doesn't know what's really happening. He needs proof. If he could talk to Darren, maybe his story would be a start. And Darren's not like us – he still looks relatively normal.'

'Thanks, mate,' chipped in Darren, grinning.

Cameron couldn't help smiling back, but he quickly returned to being serious. 'An interview. Pictures of Darren next to the story. That's going to tell the public what they need to know – get our story across without scaring people off.'

'No. Way.' Slater shook his head furiously. 'That article couldn't smell any fishier if it was wrapped around a large cod and chips. And as for this guy being there at the base tonight, that stinks of a setup! What if he's working for Fry?'

'Oh, what, and he almost gets himself killed by that hawk thing to make his story look more convincing?'

Cameron looked to Rora. Ultimately it didn't matter what Slater said, as long as she agreed.

'Slater's right,' she declared after a further pause.

Cameron blinked at her, feeling anger and frustration surging up inside. 'We can't take the risk,' Rora told him flatly. 'We've taken a few too many of those lately, and we've got precious little to show for it.'

Cameron reeled from the double-blow. She'd shot down his idea and robbed him of the power to argue back.

Furious, he turned and stormed out.

chapter seventeen

on the record

Cameron spent the next few days mostly hanging out with his own thoughts. They weren't exactly great company, because they burned with frustration. And their main focus was Rora.

Slater's opposition was entirely expected. No matter how good Cameron proved himself on missions, Slater would always be opposed to anything he suggested. But Rora's attitude had come as a real blow. He had hoped for more from her. Leaders were supposed to have vision, and at the moment she seemed unable to look at the bigger picture – the future. She was too concerned with day-to-day survival. That was vital, of course, but the monsters in the Republic needed to do more than just survive. They deserved to *live*. And for that they needed freedom. And for freedom, they needed the truth to come out, for Fry to be exposed.

Maybe he was being unreasonable, hoping for too much. Maybe Slater and Rora were only being realistic. But Cameron didn't think so. Back at school, on the footie team, he would never go out on the field aiming for a draw. He went out to score for his side. The team went out to win.

These were the kinds of thoughts that crowded his head everywhere he went. Whether he was sitting in the dining hall, pushing his food around his plate, or patrolling the upper tunnels, or beating up the punch bag in the gym. The monsters were stuck here. Cornered. To Cameron, it seemed like the walls were closing in. They weren't short of space, but what they were running out of was *time*. The army was out there, still hunting for them. Their food supply was dwindling . . .

To try to take his mind off things, Cameron went to see Darren each day. He was sharing a room with Jace while they recovered, so Cameron could chat with them both for a bit. They quickly grew tired, but the truth was, as glad as he was to have Darren safe and getting well, Cameron was too preoccupied to enjoy small talk anyway. Rora did make a few attempts at conversation, but he would always find himself responding coldly, and she soon got the picture and walked away.

Late at night on the third day, Cameron was on patrol near the surface. He'd tried going to bed early the night before, only to end up awake and brooding, so today he'd asked to be assigned a late-night patrol instead. He plucked Austin's card out of his pocket and turned it round between his fingers. He had already stored the number in his computerized memory, but it was useful to have the object there in his hand, flipping it over and over as he worked his way towards a decision.

Rora's heart might be in the right place, but if they continued to play things her way, there could only be one outcome. And it wouldn't be a draw.

Cameron tucked the card away again and brought up the number on his HUD.

Issuing the command with a thought, he dialled.

There was a tense wait while the phone rang at the other end. Cameron couldn't shake off the same feeling he had had just before the break-in at the supermarket – that he was about to do something criminal. But even if Rora was furious, that didn't make it wrong. *You're doing the right thing*, he told himself firmly.

If only he could be *sure*.

'Jack Austin.'

The journalist's tone was business-like, but just hearing his voice was a relief. If the call had gone to voicemail, Cameron knew he would probably have backed out.

'It's me,' he said. Then, realizing that he had never actually given the reporter his name, he remembered what he'd said at the memorial service when Austin had asked who he was, he added, 'The monster.'

Cameron could almost hear the wry smile in the voice on the other end of the line. 'It's good to hear from you. Thanks again – you know, for the other night.'

'Can we talk?'

'Of course. Any time. But probably best not over the phone, eh?'

'My thoughts exactly,' said Cameron. He was safe from being overheard by other monsters: the phone conversation was playing directly into his ear and he was keeping his voice low. But he wouldn't feel comfortable talking like this for any length of time. And besides, he wanted to be able to see the man's face, to be sure that Austin was genuine.

'Where can we meet?' he asked.

'You name the place,' said the reporter. 'It's important it's somewhere you feel safe.'

Cameron nodded, thinking it over. The guy was being reasonable and as helpful as he could. Did that mean he could be trusted? Or did that just make him too good to be true?

There was only one way to find out.

* * *

There was no sense in trying to sneak past Guard – even if Cameron took one of the minor exit tunnels, Guard would see him on the monitors – so he just strode out through the main entrance, muttering something about hunting rabbits. Guard probably wouldn't think much of it. The alarm would only be raised if Slater or Rora noticed him missing, but they were avoiding Cameron about as keenly as he was avoiding them. They probably wouldn't even notice he was gone.

It was past one in the morning when Cameron arrived at the roadside service station car park a couple of miles out of town that he had chosen as the meeting place. His family had always ended up stopping here after road trips, his sister Shannon complaining that she was hungry and unwilling to wait the extra few minutes it would take to get home and have Mum cook something. Cameron couldn't help thinking about those times and all that he had lost. He would never have imagined he could miss his dad nagging him to finish his homework, or his sister hogging the bathroom, but he did. The absence of these simple, everyday things – things that had been taken away from him by Doctor Fry – was sometimes what hurt the most.

From the corner of the car park, a green Prius flashed its headlights, and Cameron's thoughts snapped back to the present as Jack Austin popped the door open. Tugging his hood around his face, Cameron hurried over and jumped in.

'Everything OK?' asked Austin.

'Fine,' Cameron assured him. They sat there in silence for a short while, Cameron's gaze drifting out across the car park. At this time of night, the place wasn't busy, but there was just enough traffic in and out to ensure that nobody would pay any attention to a vehicle parked on its own.

Cameron took a deep breath.

'We haven't been properly introduced. My name's Cameron.'

Austin smiled. 'Hi, Cameron.' He produced a miniature tape recorder and planted it on top of the dashboard. 'OK if I record?'

Cameron nodded. He wasn't completely comfortable about it, but he reminded himself that this was what he was here for. To tell his story.

'I thought you might want to know a bit more about me before we get started properly,' said Austin. 'I'm sure you've been asking yourself why I'm so interested in what's been happening in Broad Harbour.'

'The question had crossed my mind,' replied Cameron, relieved that Austin had brought the subject up himself.

'I'm an independent investigative journalist,' explained Austin, settling back into his seat. 'That means I don't work for a newspaper or a TV company. I have to find my own stories. I've done a couple of undercover investigations – one on a big drugs company that was dumping chemicals into a river, and one where I had to pretend to be part of a gang of football hooligans who were involved with organized crime. Most of the time I work outside the mainstream, looking into the stories that nobody else is bothering with. A lot of people think I'm nuts – that I'm always looking for a conspiracy or a cover-up.' He laughed. 'And I suppose that most of the time I am. Nine times out of ten, there's nothing. But there's always that one . . .'

'So what brought you here?' asked Cameron.

'A tip-off. One of my sources in the government told me that they had discovered some unusual payments to a scientist working out of an obscure town called Broad Harbour.'

'Doctor Fry,' breathed Cameron.

'The very same. Apparently, the payments were authorized at the highest level. So when the Prime Minister announced he was going to attend a memorial service in Broad Harbour, I figured maybe there was more going on than met the eye, so I came down to have a snoop around. Then the bomb went off and I bumped into you – and that's when I knew I was onto something big. I've been hanging around ever since, trying to piece together what's going on, without any luck. Until you turned up again the other night. I'm hoping your story will fill in some of the gaps in mine.'

Cameron nodded slowly. 'Where should I start?'

'Wherever you like. Where do you feel it began?'

'With a school trip, I suppose . . .'

It was difficult to begin with, going over the events, speaking about them to a non-monster. But as Cameron told his story, he found it all spilling out of him – the explosion, waking up with Fry looking him over, waking up again in the morgue. Then Rora's rescue mission and what he had seen as they made their break for freedom – mainly the Bloodhounds.

'Just be glad you haven't got a close-up of them on your camera,' he said, summing up his description of them.

Austin listened patiently and rarely interrupted, and then only to ask him to explain or clarify something. He didn't roll his eyes or give any other sign that Cameron's story was anything other than entirely believable.

Cameron moved on to the subject of the painful visit home that had followed his escape.

'My parents didn't recognize me. They didn't

want to know me.' He shook his head, reliving the dreadful encounter with the people who were supposed to have loved him more than anyone else. He looked at Austin, studying him for a moment. 'You treated me better than they did. I mean, you looked at me and didn't even blink.'

'Ah, but I'm a reporter. I've seen accidents and crime scenes that— Well, they were far worse than looking at you, anyway. Of course I react – it's only natural. But you learn to do it on the inside.' He paused. 'Anyway, that must have been horrible. To be chased off by your own folks.'

Cameron nodded. He went on to relate the rest of the incident, and how Rora had whisked him away into the care of the Republic.

'Yes, the Monster Republic they're talking about on the news . . .' said Austin, scratching thoughtfully at his chin. 'Those would be your friends, right? The ones who broke into the lab with you the other night? And Rora is your leader?'

Cameron bit his lip. He had wanted to stick exclusively to his own story at this stage, but he was beginning to appreciate that unless you were a castaway on a desert island, your story was always going to involve other people. And in his case, it was proving impossible to avoid mentioning the Republic. All he could do was keep the details as sketchy as possible.

He pressed on, furnishing Austin with his account of the memorial service, how he had fought to prevent a disaster, and how the bomb that had detonated had taken out one of Fry's most vicious warriors.

'And that was when you came up and shoved a camera in my face,' he finished.

'Yeah, I remember that part. I was very fond of that camera,' Austin joked. 'So what have you been doing since then? I heard there was a shootout at the supermarket last week, but the army are keeping a pretty tight lid on the details.'

'Well, for one thing, it wasn't a shootout,' replied Cameron. 'There was only one side shooting and it wasn't us. We've mostly been hiding. That whole thing at the supermarket was because we needed food.'

Cameron grimaced, wondering if he ought to be telling Austin about one of the Republic's key weaknesses. But the army must know already – they could put two and two together.

Besides, as they had gone through the interview, Cameron had grown more and more sure that Austin was genuine. His questions were fair, he was patient and understanding, and hadn't pressed Cameron on any point he had chosen to skim over or – as in the case of Marie's story – skip altogether. He liked him. More importantly, he trusted him.

Austin sighed. 'It sounds like things are tough for your Republic. And only likely to get tougher.' He drummed his fingers on the steering wheel, thinking. 'You need an ally, you know.' He met Cameron's gaze earnestly. 'Why don't you let me come and talk to your friends? It'll help to see how you're living, outcast from society, having to survive on your own. And to have more perspectives – stories to back up yours.'

Cameron frowned. 'I'm not sure that'd be a good idea.' In his mind, he could already hear Rora's furious reaction. When it wasn't being drowned out by Slater's.

'A journalist never reveals his sources,' Austin assured him. 'Besides which, we don't have to go there directly. You can blindfold me and lead me there. I don't need to know where your base is.'

Cameron looked away across the car park. He could see a few late-night travellers through the window of the roadside restaurant. Normal people with normal lives, but none of them with any idea of what the Monster Republic was really about. To them, the Republic was just another band of terrorists.

'The thing is, Cameron, I have the weapons to take on the army. Seriously.' Austin dipped his head to Cameron's eye-level, to show the sincerity in his gaze. 'Publicity – the *right* publicity, getting the true story out – that can turn the tide for you. But I can't do anything without ammunition. Your story is a great start. But it's nothing to what the *whole* story can do.'

Cameron closed his eye, trapped in doubt and uncertainty. Venturing outside to meet a reporter was one thing, but taking him back to the base was far, far more than he had planned. Slater and Rora were certain to flip. On the other hand, everything Austin had said was true – the truth was the only weapon they had against the authorities and the ever-encroaching army.

More, he felt like he'd established a connection with Austin, and he didn't want to jeopardize the relationship by refusing what was, after all, a reasonable suggestion. But at the same time, how much would he jeopardize by so blatantly defying Rora?

It was one of those decisions that was never going to get any easier, no matter how long he thought about it.

So maybe he should just bite the bullet.

The control room was dark as Rora and Slater

hurried in. Cameron waited, leaning against one of the desks.

'What have you been doing, Cameron?' Rora demanded angrily. 'Guard said you went out *hours* ago. I was just about to send out a search party. We were worried sick.'

'Well, some of us were,' remarked Slater snidely.

'Shut up.'

Rora fixed her eyes on Cameron, making an effort to soften her tone. 'All I'm saying is, none of us should be out alone right now.'

'I wasn't alone,' Cameron confessed. 'I was with a friend.'

Rora frowned. 'What do you mean? No one else is out there.'

Cameron pulled himself upright.

'Rora, there's someone I'd like you to meet.' He half turned and beckoned to the shadowed corner behind him.

Slowly, hesitantly, a man stepped into view.

'This is Jack Austin.'

chapter eighteen

divided loyalties

For a moment nobody moved. Then, without any further warning, Slater turned, grabbed Cameron by the front of his jumper and slammed him against the rough stone wall.

'What the *hell* were you thinking?' he screamed. 'Don't bother answering! We know, don't we? You were thinking about *yourself*! You and your stupid magazine! Why didn't you just take the thing with you? Tear it up and leave a nice little paper trail right to our front door?'

Cameron stood with his arms raised, unresisting. He knew if he reacted now, the whole thing would blow up into a fight. Instead, he spoke coolly and determinedly.

'I brought Jack here blindfolded. He doesn't have a clue where we are.'

Slater fired a venomous look past Cameron, straight at the reporter.

'Really?' Then he was back glaring at Cameron. 'I suppose you scanned him for tracking devices then?'

'All I have is my tape recorder and my camera,' said Austin quietly.

'Oh well, forgive me if I don't just take your word for that!' snarled Slater, snatching up a hand-held scanner from the control desk and running it roughly over Austin's clothes. 'See, we're supposed to be in hiding, because everyone wants us *dead*. It makes us a little slow to trust strangers.'

'Anything?' asked Rora.

'He's clean,' Slater rasped. 'But what does that matter? Cameron let him bring everything else he needs for spying.' He stepped back and gestured at the door that led to the rest of the base. 'Knock yourself out, take a good look round!'

Austin didn't take him up on the invitation. Even someone who had never encountered sarcasm before would have had no trouble interpreting Slater's tone.

'Rora . . .' appealed Cameron, hoping for a more reasonable response from her at least. It was a thin hope, because her eyes blazed at least as ferociously as Slater's.

'Don't, Cameron. Just don't!' She shot a glance at the reporter, then fixed her eyes firmly back on Cameron, as though she'd decided to pretend that Austin wasn't even there. 'It's bad enough that you storm out whenever you don't get your own way, like some spoiled child. If you're so immature that you have to go and sulk, well, I guess we could live with that. But no – no, you have to go off on your own and disobey orders!'

'But, Rora,' blurted Cameron, raising his voice, despite his efforts at restraint, 'Jack can help us! He can help the Republic! The press and the media are out there spreading lies about us. *That's* why everyone wants us dead! So isn't it about time we had someone spreading the truth? Surely you can see the benefit in that?'

'All I can see right now is you doing whatever the hell you want to!' spat Slater. 'As usual. You want your buddy rescued? You engineer an excuse so we'll all help out – and all risk our lives in the process. You want your picture in the papers? You run off and bring a reporter home with you.' He clenched a fist. 'Into our base! Our *secret* base! While the whole army is out there trying to find us!'

'I'm sorry,' said Cameron. 'But nothing was going to change with us just hiding out here. It's only ever going to get worse. You must realize that. And you read that article, didn't you, Rora? Please tell me you read it.'

'So what?' she retorted, still simmering.

'So you can see what this guy could do for us if he had the full facts.'

'Yeah!' shouted Slater. 'Sell us down the river! Which do you fancy, Cameron? Firing squad or Fry's furnace? Because those'll be our only choices when he's through with us!'

Rora stood silent, apparently prepared to let Slater vent his fury, as though this time she felt Cameron deserved everything he threw at him.

'Please,' said Cameron. 'You read the article. At least just listen to the guy who wrote it. I can't change the fact that he's here—'

'I can, soon enough,' growled Slater.

Cameron pressed on. 'So there can't be any harm in hearing him out.'

'You don't have to tell me any more than you want to,' Austin said tentatively.

'You stay out of this,' ordered Slater. 'She doesn't have to tell you *anything*! None of us do!'

Rora remained silent. Her eyes still burned with anger.

An age passed. Cameron felt like a man with his head on the execution block, waiting for the axe to fall.

'All right, I'll listen to what he has to say,' said Rora eventually.

'*What?*' Slater roared, rounding on her in disgust. 'Are you off your head, Rora? Well,

I've heard more than I need to! Count me out!'

He spun round and stormed out of the room.

Silence. Austin looked awkwardly from Cameron to Rora.

'I'm sorry. I never meant to cause such disruption. I hope you can smooth things over. Things must be difficult for you right now, what with the army, the government and the public lined up against you. I wish I could say I understood what you were going through. But I don't. How can I? I'm not a monster.' He threw in a wry glance at Cameron. 'But I *want* to understand. And I want to help the public understand. Their prejudice is only going to deepen, the longer they're fed all this propaganda about you being terrorists.'

'And you think you can change their minds?' said Rora challengingly. 'In the movies, when people see a monster, they think of it as a monster. That leads to a lot of angry mobs wielding pitchforks. And in real life, it's not much different. Except that this time the mobs can lock themselves safely in their homes and leave the army to do their work for them.'

'It's true, it's not easy to turn that kind of tide. But it can be done. You'd be surprised.'

'Would I? I liked what you wrote – in your article. But how many opinions did it change? As far as I can tell from the TV news, none. We're still public enemy number one and nobody seems to doubt that. Nobody except you.'

'Exactly,' said Austin calmly. 'That's because I was only asking questions. I didn't have any answers. All I really had was a fuzzy photo and some speculation. You can't hit the national press with that. But an article showing the truth about the Republic, told by those on the inside? That'd be gold dust.'

'Gold dust? So you're only in this for the money?' snapped Rora. 'I might have known. To you, this story is just another pay cheque. But what about us? This is our whole life we're talking about!'

Austin shook his head. 'I'm in it to find the truth. Oh, there's no doubt I'll make a name for myself. And probably a stack of cash too. But even if you don't believe that I'm on your side, the money's just another reason you should trust me. There's only something in this for me if I've got a story – a real, true story – to sell.'

Rora pursed her lips, but Cameron thought he detected the hint of a thaw in her icy stare. As he knew well, Rora had no time for bull. She liked straight talking, and Austin seemed to be giving her plenty of that. Maybe she was beginning to warm to him the way Cameron had. Austin seemed to sense it too.

'I can tell you're thinking about it. So maybe my article changed one opinion at least? We're not all bad, us "normal" people.'

Rora smiled ruefully. 'Slater would disagree, I think. But yeah, you made me think that maybe there were some good people out there. And that's the first time I've thought that in a long while.'

'I'm not saying it will be easy,' Austin said seriously. 'The way you look – that frightens people, I won't kid you on that. But if there's a story to go with the pictures, they'll start to look beneath the surface.'

Rora opened her mouth to speak, but a sudden beep drew their attention to a blinking light on one of the consoles. Cameron recognized it as the internal communications system.

'Excuse me,' Rora said, walking over to it and flicking a switch. 'Go ahead.'

Smarts's voice crackled through the speaker. 'Rora, we've got a problem with generator three.'

'All right. I'll bring Tinker to take a look.' Rora turned back to Cameron and Austin. 'I'm sorry. I guess we have to cut this short. It's probably time you were going anyway. It's nearly dawn. The rest of the Republic will be getting up soon. I'd rather they didn't find you here.'

'But he can come back, can't he?' asked Cameron quickly.

'I'd very much like to,' added Austin.

'We'll see,' said Rora. 'I need to think it over.'

'But—'

'I said, *we'll see*.' Rora's tone brooked no further discussion. 'Take him out, Cameron. And make sure he doesn't see anything. I'm going to have enough trouble with Slater as it is . . .'

Cameron walked Austin back to the exit. In his hands he held the blindfold he had improvised from a rag that Austin normally used for wiping his car windscreen. He wrung and stretched the cloth awkwardly, reluctant to put it back on the reporter and take him out when so little had been accomplished.

'I'm sorry,' he said to Austin. 'I knew there'd be . . . well, difficulties. But I thought we'd make more headway than that. And as for Slater—'

'Hey,' said Austin. 'Don't worry about it. It's progress. Your friend Rora gave us a "We'll see". That's a lot better than a "No comment". And Slater? After what Fry and the world has done to you, I'm surprised you're not all as angry as he is.'

'Maybe we are. We just don't all show it the way he does.'

'Which is exactly the kind of thing I need to write about.'

'Well, I hope you get the chance.'

Jack smiled and proffered a hand. Cameron accepted the handshake gratefully. Maybe the reporter was right – maybe they had made progress.

They would just have to wait and see.

chapter nineteen

waiting game

Over the next few days Cameron took care to be on his best behaviour. He knew he had a lot to make up for before he was back in Rora's good books. So he tackled some routine maintenance tasks, making himself useful around the base, and was extra careful not to broach the subject of Austin again.

He didn't have to make any special effort to avoid Slater, because Slater was deliberately steering clear of him. The one time they did bump into each other in one of the mine passages, Slater barged past without a word. A number of other monsters seemed shy of Cameron's company too. Crawler scuttled out of any room as soon as Cameron entered it, while others cast nervous glances at him wherever he went. It reminded him of the first time he had come to the Republic, when almost everyone had given him a wide berth, not sure what to make of him.

'It's not you,' Freddy explained eagerly when Cameron raised the subject as they were fixing a leaky water pipe. Jace was still recovering from his bullet wound, and in the absence of the other half of his double act, Freddy was talking to anyone. Endlessly. 'Well, not *just* you. They're all jumpy. Slater's got them convinced it's the end of the world.'

'The end of the world?' That struck Cameron as a shade extreme, even for Slater.

'Well, OK. The end of the Republic. He's sure that reporter's going to bring something bad down on us, anyway.'

Cameron shook his head. 'Well, you know Slater. He's such a cheerful optimist.'

Freddy grinned and handed him the wrench. He lowered his voice to a whisper, even though there were no other work crews in this stretch of tunnel.

'I heard that him and Rora have been having big fights. He keeps demanding to know what she said to the reporter, and she won't tell him. And when the leaders are at each other's throats, the troops are bound to be worried.'

Cameron nodded. That was the sorry truth. Divisions could easily start to spread – like cracks in a pipe. He passed the wrench back to Freddy. Their work was done.

If only their other problems could be mended so easily.

Luckily, one of the things that *was* mending relatively smoothly was Darren. According to Tinker, that had more to do with his own natural resilience than any accelerated healing ability that Fry had given him. As far as anyone knew, Cameron was the only monster to have been given that modification.

Saying goodbye to Freddy, Cameron made his way down to Darren's room. His friend was sitting up on the top bunk flicking through a comic cradled in the crook of his broken arm.

'Hey, Cam!'

'Hey, Darren. Where's Jace?'

'He's gone up for some fresh air. Tinker says he needs to stretch his legs.'

'How are you feeling?' Cameron asked.

'Pretty good. Tired, but the burns are getting better.' Darren lifted the bandage that covered one half of his face. The skin beneath still looked sore, but not the angry, blistered red it had been when Darren had arrived at the base. 'Tinker says if I'm lucky it might not even scar.'

'Cool.' Cameron managed a half-smile.

'Oh, sorry, mate,' Darren's face was suddenly stricken. 'I didn't think – I mean, maybe your scars will, um, get better too . . .'

Cameron snorted. 'It's OK, Darren. I know I'm stuck with what I've got. I'm used to it now.'

He took a deep breath. Darren seemed calm, Jace wasn't around – maybe this was the moment to bring up the subject they both seemed to have been avoiding . . .

'Anyway, *I* should be apologizing to *you*. If I hadn't got you mixed up in all this, then Fry wouldn't have burned your house down and . . . and your mum would still be alive. I'm really sorry.'

Darren nodded vaguely.

'It's OK, Cam,' he said. 'I don't remember much about it, to be honest. Everything seems a bit of a blur, until I woke up here.'

'But you must—' Cameron cut himself off before he could say 'miss your mum'. He remembered the pain he had felt in the days after his own parents had rejected him. He didn't want to inflict the same pain on Darren. Perhaps Darren's memories would clear in time, or maybe he was just dealing with grief his own way. Cameron didn't feel like he had the right to interfere.

'Anyway,' he said, putting on a cheerful grin, 'I should probably be going. Rora's bound to have something for me to do. But I'll come back and see you in a bit, yeah?'

'Yeah,' replied Darren with a yawn. 'Laters.'

With a wave, Cameron headed down towards

204

the dining hall. It was almost dinner time, and Rora was bound to be there. His brief chat with Darren had been enough to boost Cameron's confidence. He'd handled one difficult conversation; maybe it was time to tackle another . . .

He found the fox-girl sitting at one end of a long table, picking at a plate of vegetable stew. More encouragingly, she was scanning the magazine. Knowing Rora, it wouldn't be the lipstick ads that had her attention, so he could only assume she was re-reading the article. It was the perfect opportunity. Or at least the best he was likely to get.

'Mind if I sit down?' he asked.

'It's a free country,' she said, with heavy irony. She set the magazine down on the table in front of her as Cameron sat opposite. 'What's on your mind? As if I didn't know.'

Her tone was cool, but it held no real anger, as it had done in the first couple of days after Austin's visit. Cameron tried to take that as an encouraging sign.

'Listen,' he began. 'I've got a suggestion. But

I'm not going off and doing my own thing without consulting you.'

'I'm glad to hear it,' she replied, with the barest trace of a smile.

'It's been four days since Austin was here. And I know Slater's been spouting doom and gloom, but nothing's happened. I can't help thinking that if – well, if Austin was any kind of spy, then the army or the Bloodhounds or someone would have been knocking on our door by now.'

'You may be right.' Rora sat up, resting her arms on the table. 'What's your point, Cameron?'

'Well, Darren's getting better. He's probably well enough to do an interview. And unlike the memorial service and the power plant explosion, the fire at his house was never linked to us in the news. So if Darren can connect that to Fry, it'll help cast doubt on the other incidents.'

'Maybe.' Rora seemed determined to make him work for this. 'So what are you suggesting?'

'That Austin comes back for another visit.'

Cameron swallowed, his throat suddenly quite dry.

'Hmm,' said Rora. She steepled her hands and tapped her fingers against each other. 'It's a risk, but you're right – if he could have brought trouble to us, I think he would have done it by now.'

'I'll give him a call, then,' said Cameron. He kept his voice even, but inside he wanted to whoop with joy.

'OK,' replied Rora. 'But remember, just because he hasn't double-crossed us yet, that doesn't mean he doesn't *want* to. Make absolutely sure he doesn't know where he's coming. Get Tinker to give you a scanner to check him for bugs and bring him in blindfolded, just like before.'

Cameron nodded. He didn't want to ask the next question, but he felt he had to.

'What about Slater?'

Rora put a hand on his arm and looked into his eyes. 'Listen, you leave Slater to me. You need to concentrate on what you're doing. I don't want you to put yourself in danger by worrying about him. Just be careful out there.'

'Always.' He smiled.

Rora smiled back, her hand lingering on his arm for a moment. Then she dropped her eyes and cleared her throat.

'OK – off you go then.'

Despite Rora's concern, Cameron had no difficulty in getting Austin back to the base. Meeting him at their previous rendezvous point in the car park, the reporter had made no protest as Cameron scanned him for tracking devices (none found) and retied the makeshift blindfold over his eyes. They had taken a roundabout route back to the base, and Cameron was confident there was no way Austin could have kept track of where they were.

Rora was waiting for them just inside the main gate. Austin blinked as Cameron removed the blindfold, then smiled warmly and shook her hand.

'Thank you for this,' he said. 'I know it must

have been a tough decision.'

'Just don't make me regret it,' answered Rora, sounding guarded.

If Austin was fazed by the cool reception, though, he didn't show it.

'I'll do whatever I can to earn your trust.' He fished his tape recorder out of his coat pocket. 'Where would you like me to start? Cameron says I should talk to his friend Darren . . .'

Rora nodded. 'That's right. He's waiting in the dining hall. Cameron'll take you there.'

Cameron raised his eyebrow.

'You're not coming?'

'Generator three has broken down *again*. I have to go and talk to Smarts. I'll catch you up.'

'OK. This way.'

As Cameron ushered Austin past, Rora shot him a look which was half *Welcome back*, half *Are you OK to take care of this?* and he returned a small nod.

Leaving Rora behind, Cameron led Austin through the dimly lit warren of tunnels.

'Not exactly five-star accommodation, is it?'

muttered Austin.

'Luxury isn't a priority when you're in hiding,' replied Cameron.

'I can see that. Where is everybody?'

Apart from Rora, there had been no sign of anyone else since they had entered the base. Cameron suspected that the other monsters were keeping well out of the way of this mysterious and potentially dangerous guest.

'Um, working probably,' he explained. 'Here we are.'

As they turned a corner, they found Slater standing guard at the door of the dining hall. He greeted Austin with a sniff, his expression a clear warning. Cameron ignored him and led the way through the door, keen to get Austin out of Slater's disapproving glare as quickly as possible.

Darren stood up as they entered.

'Hi,' he said. He had taken the bandages off his face, and he looked young and nervous. 'I'm Darren. You're not going to be putting my picture in the paper, are you?'

'What's the matter?' prodded Cameron.

'Since when did you worry about what you looked like?'

'Since I've seen myself in the mirror.'

'Relax.' Austin grinned. 'We'll save the painful photo shoot till later. I'm Jack Austin, by the way.' He sat down across the table from Darren and placed his tape recorder between them. 'Anyway, I haven't decided whether to use your picture or Cameron's.'

Darren smirked. 'Oh, no contest. I was always better looking than him.'

He fired Cameron a wink, and for a moment it was like they were back at school again, trading mock insults. Again Cameron felt a surge of relief that Darren hadn't blamed him for what had happened.

'So,' began Austin. 'Tell me your story . . .'

chapter twenty
internal investigations

The interview was quick and smooth. After all, Darren's story was simpler than Cameron's. The only sticky moment came when Austin asked him to describe the fire at his house. For a moment Darren seemed to freeze, his eyes filling with anger and pain. Then, as quickly as the look had come, it vanished, replaced by glazed bewilderment.

'I don't remember much,' he said quietly. 'It happened at night. I was in bed. I think the smell of smoke woke me up. The fire was already on the landing, but I managed to make it down the stairs. Then I think I must've blacked out. I don't remember anything until I woke up here.'

Austin pursed his lips, a tiny crease appearing between his eyebrows. Cameron shifted awkwardly. He hoped the reporter wasn't going to press Darren too much. But it turned out he needn't have worried. Austin quickly changed the subject, closing the interview with an easy question about how Darren was finding life as part of the Monster Republic.

'Well, that was relatively painless.' Darren smiled as Austin clicked off his tape recorder. 'I think I'll be able to cope with the fame, as long as I don't get mobbed by autograph hunters.'

Cameron laughed. 'Oh yeah. That's a *major* problem with being a monster, I find.'

'What are you doing next?' asked Darren.

'Well, I was hoping to see a bit more of the base,' said Austin. 'Would that be OK, Cameron?'

Cameron grimaced. 'I'm not sure. Rora might not—'

'Oh, come on, Cam,' interrupted Darren. 'I haven't seen half of this place yet. Let's have a tour!'

'Would you be up to that?' asked Austin immediately. 'Are you sure you're well enough?'

'I don't see why not,' said Cameron sarcastically. 'He's been lazing in bed ever since he got here. But listen—'

'Lead the way, mate,' Darren cut in again. 'And try to spice up the commentary. I don't want this to be as "interesting" as old Hackford's field trip to the Broad Harbour Museum of Anchors and Maritime History!'

Cameron laughed. It was good to hear his friend's familiar jokey tone. Surely it couldn't hurt to show him and Austin around a bit? After all, even if the reporter could somehow memorize the whole layout of the base, it was no use to him if he didn't know where the entrance was.

'Come on, then.' He grinned. 'But don't think we're going slowly just 'cos you're crocked . . .'

Careful to avoid any obviously sensitive areas, like the power generators and Tinker's workshop, Cameron led the pair on a quick tour of the kitchens, living quarters and finally the rec room. There, he was able to introduce Austin to some of the other monsters, including Freddy and Smarts, who were playing chess (Smarts beating Freddy on five boards simultaneously). There was still no sign of Crawler, which Cameron thought was probably just as well – the angry, many-armed boy might be a bit too much to handle, even for the understanding Austin – but he was able to introduce both Darren and Austin to Digger, a young lad with steel, rodent-like teeth and great shovel-shaped hands, who was watching an old Jackie Chan film on the battered plasma screen Tinker had salvaged from a skip and fixed up not long after they had moved into the base.

However, the rooms and tunnels of the base were largely empty. Most of the monsters were still making themselves scarce. Cameron wondered if they were acting on Rora's orders

215

– he knew she didn't want to give Austin too accurate an idea of how many monsters were in the Republic – or whether, rather like Slater, they preferred not to have anything to do with the visiting journalist.

As the trio passed the door to the control room, though, Cameron finally spotted a familiar face. He turned to Austin.

'One more quick stop. There's someone else who's very keen to meet you.'

Tinker was seated at one of the consoles, scanning the monitor in front of him, but he spun round in his chair as they all filed in.

He seemed more jittery than usual, wiping his palm on his trousers and holding out his hand, like a nervous fan about to meet his favourite footballer.

'Tinker,' announced Cameron, 'this is Jack Austin. He's the guy I was telling you about.'

'H-h-h-h-h-hi,' managed Tinker.

'Tinker's an admirer of your handiwork at Fry's lab – the hole in the fence,' explained Cameron.

'I c-c-could tell it w-was a p-p-prof-f-fessional

job,' Tinker forced out. 'V-v-very n-nicely d-d-done.'

'It was nothing much,' said Austin, with a modest shrug. 'In my line of work, it helps to know a bit about security systems. I've picked up some bits and pieces over the years.' He gestured around the room. 'I'm impressed with your setup here. You've got electricity, water, heating – it's incredible what you've achieved. And Cameron tells me that you're the technical expert behind it all.'

Tinker blushed lobster-red at the unexpected praise. 'I h-h-have a lot of h-h-help. Smarts does a lot of the d-d-designing with me.'

'And security must be a *nightmare*. What kind of system do you have rigged?' asked Austin casually.

'W-w-well, we have video feeds at fixed points at the entrance and around the perimeter,' answered Tinker, clearly thrilled to be talking with a kindred spirit. 'They're triggered by m-m-motion sensors. I— Oh . . .'

Tinker's face dropped like a stone. 'Maybe I shouldn't be t-t-telling you all this.'

Austin held up his hands at once. 'Sorry. I didn't mean to pry. I'm not trying to steal your state secrets.'

Cameron chuckled. Anyone could see that Austin wasn't prying, he was just interested.

'It's OK, go ahead,' he told Tinker. 'Only, like the man says – no state secrets.'

Cameron walked over to Darren as Tinker and Austin started talking shop on security matters. Tinker was in his element, even casting off his stutter as he waxed lyrical on the topic of motion sensors, closed-circuit TV and various other electronic precautions that he had either installed personally or supervised with his expert eye. Cameron turned to share a joke with his friend, but Darren was listening intently as Tinker demonstrated where the feeds from the motion sensors led into the security camera system. He had an expression of surprised wonder on his face, like he was struggling to take it all in.

'Impressive, isn't it?' Cameron said quietly.

'It's well cool,' replied Darren, his eyes still darting everywhere. 'I had no idea you had all this computer kit down here. It's like the lair in some Bond movie.'

'Except that we're not the bad guys, remember?' Cameron said, digging his elbow into Darren's ribs.

'What the hell is going on here?'

Rora stood in the doorway with a face like thunder, her eyes locked on Austin and Tinker. At her shoulder was Slater, ever the loyal lieutenant.

Cameron raised his hands in a calming gesture. 'Don't panic. We're just talking about general electronics and stuff. No harm done.'

'I think I'll be the judge of that, thanks,' said Rora, her expression a sharp reminder of who was in charge.

Slater took two quick steps into the room and laid a beefy hand on Austin's shoulder.

'Come on, mate,' he growled. 'Time you were going.'

'Take your hands off him,' snapped Cameron.

Slater cocked his head challengingly.

'Make me.'

Cameron squared up to the taller boy,

setting his shoulders aggressively.

'Now wait—' began Rora.

An alarm shrieked.

Already tense, Cameron practically jumped out of his skin. Rora looked shocked, Slater disappointed. Tinker spun to face a bank of monitors lining one wall, hastily flicking switches.

'Tinker?' Guard's agitated voice barked over the speaker. 'Come in, Tinker!'

Cameron knew the note of panic was a very bad sign. Guard never panicked.

'G-G-Guard, tell me where to look!'

'East slope. There's an army patrol. They're heading right for us!'

chapter twenty-one

red alert

Tinker's hands flew over the controls, conjuring a selection of views on the monitors in front of him. Rora and Cameron closed in behind, peering over his shoulder. In one shot, Cameron could make out jeeps and trucks moving along the road. The number of vehicles was enough to tell him that the army was present in considerable force. Cameron could see they were nearby too, but he couldn't remember the precise locations of all the cameras the way Tinker did.

'How close are they?'

'Ab-b-b-out five hundred metres f-f-from Tunnel Th-Three.'

Cameron nodded tightly. That was a ventilation shaft. It was reasonably well concealed by an overgrown fringe of grass, but if the soldiers got out of their vehicles to conduct a thorough sweep, they were unlikely to mistake it for a rabbit burrow.

'Check the other entrances,' commanded Rora.

'There's n-no need. The m-m-motion sensors would have tri-triggered the other c-c-c-cameras.'

'Do it anyway.'

'She's right, Tinker,' said Austin. 'If they have your location, they'll be covering every exit as they close the net.'

With a roar of fury, Slater pulled Austin away from the screen and shook him violently.

'How did you do it, then?' he yelled. 'Eh?! Tracking device? GPS on your phone? *What?!*'

'Get off me!' snapped Austin, angry and taken aback. He flexed his arms, pulling himself free of Slater's grip. Unfortunately,

Slater seemed to take that as an attack and swung a fist. Rora's hand flashed out and deflected his arm before the punch landed.

'Slater!' she practically screamed at him. Now Austin's fists were up in a defensive pose and Rora turned her anger on him too.

'Back off! I mean it, both of you!' She shot furious looks from one to the other. 'I want some distance between you two – right now!'

'That's fine!' declared Slater. 'I want plenty of distance – I want this traitor out of here!'

'I haven't betrayed anyone!' insisted Austin.

Cameron watched tensely as Slater and Austin glared at each other, Rora's small figure wedged between them. He wanted to leap to the reporter's defence. Just because the soldiers were here, it was totally unfair to jump to the conclusion that Austin had something to do with it. For a split-second, he wondered if he should try to help Rora restrain Slater, but he knew that would only aggravate the situation. Cameron was the last person Slater would want laying hands on him.

'T-t-two h-hundred m-m-metres!' Tinker called,

punching buttons and flicking switches as he activated other cameras dotted around the various tunnel entrances.

Slater, his fist still clenched even though Rora had hold of his arm, bared his teeth in an ugly snarl. Austin maintained his defensive stance, as though expecting Slater to fly at him at any moment. Darren stood rooted to the spot, looking like he'd rather be anywhere else.

Cameron knew how he felt.

'Did everyone hear that?' he said. 'Two hundred metres. Hadn't we better think about, I don't know, getting out of here, rather than fighting each other?'

Nobody answered.

'One h-h-hundred m-m-metres,' said Tinker.

'They're almost here,' Cameron said through gritted teeth.

But it seemed that no one was listening. Cameron wondered what on earth he could say to break the deadlock and get people not only paying attention but taking action. He could see that Rora at least wanted to be moving, but she obviously felt trapped, all her efforts required just keeping the peace.

'W-w-wait!' Tinker held up his hand. He flicked through several views of the same group of jeeps. 'Yes! I th-think they're m-moving on!'

'What?' said Rora, only half turning her head so she could still keep an eye on the stand-off between Slater and Austin.

Cameron leaned in over Tinker, checking the scene outside for himself. The convoy of vehicles had passed the narrow track that led up the hill to the mine entrance and was continuing along the road to Broad Harbour.

'They're leaving,' said Cameron. He breathed a huge sigh of relief. 'Must have been another new patrol route. They weren't coming for us after all.'

'It m-makes sense,' said Tinker. 'We know they're always ch-ch-changing their p-p-patrol p-p-patterns.'

'It's what I would do *if* I had anything to do with the army,' said Austin with pointed emphasis. 'Keep the enemy guessing and see if I could scare some of them out of hiding.'

Slater snatched his arm free of Rora's grasp, but said nothing. Rora allowed herself to relax a degree or two. She faced Austin.

'Well, whatever they're trying to do, it's time you were going. As soon as the coast is clear, Cameron can take you back.'

'Wait,' put in Cameron, moving to Austin's side. 'He had nothing to do with it!'

'Says you,' retorted Slater.

'It doesn't matter anyway.' Rora met Cameron's gaze briefly, and the unspoken apology told him what was coming next. 'I'm sorry, Mr Austin, but I think we need to call a halt to the interviews.'

'Oh, now wait,' said Austin, shaking his head in dismay. 'I don't have nearly enough information yet if I'm going to do the article. And I need photos.'

'He didn't even get to take my picture,' offered Darren quietly.

But Rora wasn't about to budge.

'Like I said, I'm sorry. But if the patrols are moving closer to the base, we can't risk any unnecessary activity. I know the article might do us some good eventually, but we're going to have to put it on hold. The truth can wait.'

'No!' protested Austin. 'If time is running out for you, then we need to get your story out sooner, not later. Later will be too late.'

'Rora,' pleaded Cameron, desperately searching her gaze for some sign that she could be swayed, 'you're giving up our best chance to get back at Fry. Maybe our only chance.'

But her eyes were cold, her decision plainly set in stone.

'When the coast is clear,' she repeated, 'you take him home. And you stay out of contact until I say so – is that understood?'

Cameron bit his tongue. Slater's head was up and his arms were folded. His face wore a smug sneer, like he'd won something. But there was no point in arguing.

'Fine,' said Cameron. 'You're the boss.'

He led Austin back to the main entrance in silence, Slater shadowing them both all the way. As Guard looked on impassively, the reporter deliberately turned his back on Slater as Cameron tied on his blindfold.

'Wait!' said Slater as Cameron made to lead Austin out.

Swaggering forward, the dog-legged monster made a show of checking the blindfold was securely fastened.

'OK,' he smirked finally. 'See you around.'

Swallowing a sharp reply, Cameron guided Austin out. They made the long journey back to the car park in silence. There didn't seem to be anything left to say. Only when they were back beside the Prius and Austin had tugged off his blindfold did the reporter speak.

'She's wrong, you know.'

Cameron lowered his head. 'I know.'

'I *need* that information,' Austin sighed. 'Without it . . .'

'I'm sorry,' said Cameron. 'When things have calmed down a bit, maybe we can carry on.'

'Maybe.' Austin looked Cameron dead in the eye. 'I just hope for your sake that by then it isn't too late . . .'

chapter twenty-two

betrayed

'Rora wants to see you.'

Cameron blinked himself awake. Freddy stood in the doorway of his room, shifting awkwardly from foot to foot.

'Yeah? Well, I don't want to see her.'

Cameron checked the clock on his HUD: 5.57 a.m. Great.

'Tell her we have nothing to talk about,' he said.

'Uh, OK.' Freddy nodded once and left.

After dropping Austin off at the car park, Cameron had returned to the base, heading straight for bed. He hadn't bothered going back to the control room to see Rora. He knew they would only end up arguing, so what was the point? He rolled over on his narrow bunk, the wooden slats groaning in protest, and closed his good eye again. He'd known she wouldn't let it lie, but if she wanted to give him another hard time, she could wait until after breakfast.

She didn't wait five minutes.

In a crackle of static that jerked him fully awake, her voice burst into his head.

'Cameron, get up here *now*.'

Cameron swore. She must have got Tinker to patch directly through to his internal communicator. He wanted to tell her where to go, but something in her tone suggested that wouldn't be a good idea.

'Fine,' he snapped. Cutting the connection, he pulled himself out of bed, threw on some clothes and headed for the control room.

Rora and Tinker were waiting for him, leaning over a table that stood next to one of the big banks of complicated-looking equipment whose purpose Cameron had never quite been sure of. Slater was pacing to and fro in the background, the expression of self-satisfied smugness Cameron had last seen on his face replaced by cold fury.

'What is it?'

Rora raised her head. She looked steamed too. Really, *really* mad. Tinker was visibly trembling.

'This,' she said, pointing.

Laid out in front of them was a small electronic device about the size and shape of a child's frisbee. Cameron had a good idea what it was, but he wasn't in any mood to help Rora out.

So he shrugged. Rora's face hardened.

As if hoping to prevent an explosion, Tinker jumped in.

'It's a m-m-motion sensor. After our c-c-close call yesterday, I thought I'd b-b-better run a f-f-full check on the security system. Th-th-this sensor activates a n-number of k-k-key c-c-cameras c-c-covering the old v-v-ventilation shaft.'

'So what's it doing here?'

'What do you think, genius?' growled Slater. 'It's been messed with.'

He grabbed the sensor from the table and turned it round so that Cameron could see where a small panel had been removed from the black casing, revealing a compact cluster of wires. Two of the wires had been pulled loose, their frayed copper ends exposed. 'What do you think of your reporter buddy now?'

Cameron stared into the three accusing faces opposite him.

'You think Austin had something to do with this?' he said incredulously. 'I don't see how that's possible. He was never out of my sight.'

'Then maybe he came back when we weren't looking,' said Slater.

'It could have been done after he left,' agreed Rora. 'We know he's skilled at intrusion. And he could easily have a better idea of our location than he let on. Either he wants his story so badly he was ready to sneak back in to get it, or it's something worse. Whatever his reasons, it means he can't be trusted.'

'Wait, wait,' said Cameron, picturing Austin's friendly, open face. It just didn't fit with the betrayal. 'What about the soldiers? Couldn't one of them have disabled it somehow? Maybe that sweep was a diversion – keep us focused on them while somebody tampered with the sensor.'

'Oh yeah!' said Slater, slapping his forehead. 'Of course! Or maybe the man in the moon came down last night with his wire clippers and did the job while we were all sleeping. Come off it! If the soldiers had anything to do with this they'd have been storming our tunnels yesterday. Don't be so dense! It was him!'

Cameron felt heat rising in his face. But it wasn't Slater's abuse that smarted – the sting came from a growing anger at the thought that Austin had fooled him so completely. He wanted to deny it, wanted the others to be wrong, but the more he ran their argument through his mind, the less he could argue with it. There was no other explanation.

Cameron's heart sank, turning to lead in his chest as he remembered how interested Austin had been in the security system. How he and Tinker had chatted about it so animatedly right here in the control room. Right in front of him, for God's sake. The reporter had even seen the system in action when the soldiers approached.

He knew now why Rora's eyes blazed with such accusation. He was the one who had persuaded her to let Austin in. It was his fault. He had trusted Austin and the reporter had paid him back with this. That fired an even harsher anger in him. The sense of betrayal cut as sharp and deep as Fry's scalpels.

Furious, Cameron snatched the sensor from Slater's hand, spun about and marched for the door.

'Cameron!' called Rora. 'Where do you think you're going?'

'To find Austin,' he said. 'I'll give him an interview he'll never forget.'

It took Cameron's computer-enhanced brain less than ten seconds to pluck Austin's address from the Internet. By the time he was out of the base, he already had a route plotted. As he emerged into the half-light of dawn, he broke into a sprint. Picking up speed, he raced across the hillside, his power-driven legs pounding the earth as they ate up the ground between him and the reporter, his mind full of ugly thoughts.

The streets of Broad Harbour were empty. It was too early for anyone but the milkman to be out and about, and Cameron made his way unchallenged to the street where Austin lived. He stood for a moment, staring at the small terraced house. It looked so innocent – blue front door, pale curtains, neat front garden – but Cameron knew better than most that appearances could be deceptive. A single light burned in an upstairs window. It seemed that Jack Austin was an early riser. Or had he been working away all night, tapping out more of the lies he had used to worm his way into Cameron's confidence? Or maybe he'd only just got back from a midnight return trip to the Republic's secret base . . .

Anger swelling again in his chest, Cameron crossed the road to the door. One sharp push with his mechanized muscles was enough to force the lock. The door gave with a low splintering sound, and he was inside. His footsteps sounded heavy on the stairs. Heavy enough to draw Austin out of his room and onto the landing. The reporter looked shocked – unshaven and wild-haired.

'Jeez, Cameron, it's you. What the hell are you doing here?'

Cameron didn't answer. Reaching the top of the stairs, he shoved Austin back into the room he'd emerged from. The reporter stumbled, half falling onto a battered old sofa. Cameron followed him in.

'Cameron, what's going on?'

'Where were you last night?'

Austin's face was a picture of bewilderment. 'Right here. Writing up the notes from my interview with Darren. I've been up all night.'

Cameron tossed the motion sensor into Austin's lap.

'So I suppose you're going to tell me you don't know anything about this.'

Austin looked down at the device. He picked it up and turned it over a few times in his hands. Then he looked up at Cameron's furious face and swallowed nervously, as if he had finally worked out why he was there, and quite how easy it would be for Cameron to kill him.

'I know it's an SVMS-234C motion sensor, and I know a lot about its technical specifications – which probably wouldn't mean much to you.' He lifted it to his eye, paying particular attention to the exposed wires. 'I can also tell you it's been tampered with.'

'What?' said Cameron. 'You're admitting it?'

'Admitting what?' replied Austin.

With a snarl, Cameron swept his mechanical arm across Austin's desk.

'Don't play stupid!'

Austin cringed as a laptop computer, a lamp and several thick folders crashed against the far wall.

'Camer—'

'I trusted you,' Cameron spat. 'How could I have been so stupid?'

Austin shook his head. 'What? You think this had something to do with me?'

'Of course it was you!' roared Cameron.

'I bring you to the base, show you the system, and the next thing I know, this happens.'

'Wait, wait, wait!' Austin pleaded. 'It wasn't me.'

'Rubbish! Who else has got the skills to do something like this?'

'Any number of people,' protested Austin. 'Security experts, police – the army.'

'Yeah, but how many of them knew where to find us?' retorted Cameron, leaning over Austin threateningly. 'Only you.'

Austin scrambled backwards into the corner of the room, his hands up, palms open.

'Cameron, listen for a minute. You haven't thought this through. If I had wanted to disable that thing, you wouldn't be here confronting me with the evidence now because – no disrespect – you would never have found it. Tinker said himself that I was an expert. What was done to that sensor was a crude, quick bit of sabotage.'

Cameron hesitated. He hadn't thought of it like that. He stared at the reporter, pressed against the wall as if he wanted to get as far away as possible from the psychopathic monster who had broken into his home. Austin looked genuine – but then he always had. He could be as good at bluffing as he was at breaking and entering. As if he could sense Cameron's uncertainty, Austin cleared his throat and spoke again.

'Cameron, listen. The only motive for sabotaging a motion sensor would be to allow an enemy undetected access to your base, right? But to do that, the sensor would have to be disabled in such a way that the sabotage goes undiscovered until that enemy is ready to make their move. This job is so crude and obvious it might as well have a big flashing sign saying "sabotage". Besides, I didn't have an opportunity to go anywhere near the sensors – I was with you the whole time, remember? I don't even know where your base is. I know you've got every reason to be jumpy, but this time you've jumped to the wrong conclusion.'

Cameron picked up the motion sensor from where it had fallen. Austin's story made perfect sense. Tinker *had* said that Austin had disabled the alarm on the fence at the lab like a professional. If that was true, why would he do such a crude job on the motion sensor?

'But *someone* did this,' he muttered. 'If not you, then who?'

'Who else knows about the security system?' asked Austin, cautiously stepping away from the wall.

'Hardly anyone. Tinker built it, and Smarts helped design it. But he's blind – even if he could find his way to the ventilation shaft, he couldn't do this. Then there's only me, Rora and Slater.'

'And Darren,' added Austin. 'He was there yesterday when Tinker was telling me about the security system.'

'Well, yeah,' said Cameron. 'He was. But he wouldn't do something like this.'

'What makes you so sure?'

'He's my *friend*.' Cameron frowned. 'Why would Darren betray us? It doesn't make sense.'

'But you said it yourself – *someone* has to

have done it. And if it wasn't me, it has to be someone on the inside. Besides, something's been puzzling me about Darren ever since that interview with him.'

'What?'

'Well, remember when he was talking about the fire? I mean, that must have been one hell of a trauma – to be trapped inside your burning home and to lose your mum.' Austin shook his head. 'I can't even *imagine* what it would be like. But the way Darren described it, he could have been talking about a walk in the park.'

'What do you mean?'

'He just seemed too calm about it all. Too matter-of-fact. Like . . .' Austin searched for the words. 'Like he half-remembers it, but all his emotions – the shock, the loss, the grief – have been shut off. Removed.'

Cameron felt the breath leave his body as if a giant, ice-cold fist had clamped him in its grip.

Emotions removed. Memories tampered with.

His mind spun back to his own conversations

with Darren. The way his friend had avoided talking about the past. Cameron had assumed it was something Darren would get over in time. And, of course, his own guilt over what happened meant that he hadn't wanted to press the point. But what if Darren hadn't just been in some sort of denial? What if something had been done to *make* him forget? There was only one person who could do that.

Dr Lazarus Fry.

And hot on the heels of that revelation came an even more horrific thought.

What else could the doctor have done to Darren that the Republic didn't know about?

chapter twenty-three

friend or foe?

Cameron was at the door in a split-second.

'Where are you going?'

'Back to base. I think Fry has done something to Darren. I have to find him, fast.'

'Well, yes. But it'll be quicker if I give you a lift, won't it?'

That was true enough. Cameron was pretty fast – he'd been a good runner even before Fry had inflicted all his artificial enhancements on him. But the car could shave half an hour off the journey. He was just surprised that Austin was so happy to help. He had thought the guy might be hacked off about being accused of treachery.

'I won't be able to take you in with me,' Cameron warned.

'I know that. And it's OK.' Austin jumped to his feet and snatched his car keys from the desk. 'Maybe once you've dealt with this, Rora will let me come back. I'll take you as far as our meeting point.'

'Thanks.'

They hurried down the stairs and through the broken front door.

'Sorry about that,' said Cameron.

'Don't worry,' replied Austin. 'I needed a new one anyway.'

Unlocking his car, the reporter slid into the driver's seat and turned the key in the ignition. As Cameron jumped in on the passenger side, Austin hit the accelerator, steering them onto the road. Cameron sat back and buckled up. He knew he owed Austin an apology for more than just the door. But for now he was just too preoccupied with what he was going to say to his best friend.

The roads were still clear, and it took only a few minutes to reach the service station where their first secret meeting had taken place.

'Thanks again,' said Cameron as he leaped out. 'I'll be in touch as soon as I can.'

He knew Rora would have said that he shouldn't head directly for the base, but Cameron was in too much of a hurry to worry about throwing Austin off the scent. He was more convinced than ever that the reporter could be trusted.

Pushing his cybernetic limbs to the maximum, Cameron tore up the hillside, praying that he was going to be in time. As he skidded into the mine shaft and came to a halt at the main door, he saw the first indication that something was wrong – there was no sign of Guard at his usual station. A stressed-looking Freddy was manning the monitors.

'What's going on?' Cameron demanded.

'Hey, Cameron! Thank God you're back! Something's happened. You'd better go in – Rora will want to see you right away!'

Without waiting to hear more, Cameron pelted down the passage and into the main complex. He was heading straight for the control room when he ran into a cluster of monsters outside Tinker's workshop. Shoving people roughly aside, Cameron battled his way forward.

Rora met him at the door.

'What's happening?' he demanded.

'It's Guard.' The fox-girl's face was grave. 'He's hurt.'

'Oh no.' Cameron's heart sank. Pushing past Rora, he entered the workshop.

Tinker was bent over Guard's small body, the third patient in less than a month to be laid out in his chair. Behind him, Slater was chewing his fingernails, for once looking more concerned than angry. Smarts hovered at one end of the workshop, his hands twisting together anxiously.

Cameron turned to Rora. He knew what he had to ask next, even though he was dreading the answer. Just asking the question felt like a betrayal, but he had to know. He forced the words past his lips:

'Was it Darren?'

Rora nodded.

'Where is he?'

'He's gone.'

'Gone?'

'Yeah, gone,' growled Slater. 'Gone mental.'

Rora gritted her teeth and shut her eyes against Slater's tone. Evidently she wouldn't have chosen to put it in quite the same way.

'It's true,' she confirmed. 'He tried to leave the base. When Guard stopped him at the entrance, he . . . he hit him.'

'Smashed his head in with a wrench!' Slater clarified angrily. 'See for yourself.'

He stepped aside, giving Cameron an unobstructed view.

One that left him sick to his stomach.

Guard's metal skull cap had been practically caved in. His eyes, although open, were completely blank and vacant. His steel jaw hung open too. A huge dent on the left-hand side of his head suggested a blow more powerful than Cameron would have believed Darren capable of. Whether it was the product of modified muscle power or just pure unbridled aggression, he could only guess.

It made no difference. What mattered was that Guard was out cold.

Tinker was leaning over the boy, concentrating intently as he ran a slender stylus-like tool around the edges of the skull cap.

'I th-think I'm going t-t-to have to remove the whole thing. It's m-m-m-more than a simple c-c-case of hammering out the d-d-dents. M-much m-m-more.'

Rora swallowed. 'You think there might be damage to the circuitry inside?'

'S-s-serious damage.' Tinker nodded sadly, looking up at Rora with a pained expression.

Cameron couldn't take his eyes off the dent. It looked like a deep, smooth crater in the polished metal. He hated to think what might have been crushed inside.

'Is that something you can repair?'

Tinker shrugged. 'I w-w-won't know until I've opened him up.'

'I can probably design some new components and circuit boards,' said Smarts. 'But if there's damage to the brain as well ...'

Cameron felt cold. The thought of his best friend doing something so brutal was bad enough, but somehow it was worse that he had done it to Guard. The boy might have been part of Fry's Bloodhound project, but Cameron had never known him to be anything other than peaceful and quiet. He was sure Guard could have harmed someone with that steel jaw, but he never had.

'So – what happened? I mean, why did Darren suddenly blow up like this?'

'We're lucky he *didn't* blow up,' sneered Slater. 'If he'd had a bomb inside him, he could have taken a lot more of us out.'

'A b-b-bomb would have been too easily detected,' said Tinker. 'I didn't f-f-find anything like that.'

'No tracking devices either,' Rora added.

'I think Fry might have tampered with his memories,' said Cameron quietly. 'That's why he seemed so calm about what had happened to him. Is that possible?'

'For Fry?' Tinker nodded. 'Y-y-yes, I think so. And it would m-m-make sense of Darren's violent behaviour too. If Fry modified Darren's brain, he could have left s-s-something else there as well.'

'Something else?' Rora looked worried.

'Have you h-h-heard of a Trojan horse?'

Rora shook her head. Even Slater looked blank.

'It's a piece of computer p-p-programming. Like a virus.'

'What does it do?' asked Cameron.

'It allows a h-h-hacker to take control of a computer remotely. If Fry had installed one in D-D-Darren's system, it would lie dormant, impossible to d-d-detect until it was activated. But when it was, Fry would take over Darren's body completely. He'd be able to make him do whatever he w-w-wanted.'

Cameron punched a fist into his palm.

'That's what happened to the motion sensor! Fry activated the Trojan horse software to get Darren to sabotage it.'

'Why?' Slater seemed so shocked by the latest turn of events that he'd even forgotten to shout.

'So Darren could get out without being seen,' said Cameron, 'and then lead Fry back here. But when Tinker found the sabotaged motion sensor, Darren couldn't escape that way.'

'So Fry made him break out,' finished Rora.

'Which way did he go?' Cameron asked.

'Nobody saw,' said Rora, biting her lip in frustration. 'Guard might have been able to tell us, but—'

'How long's he been gone?' demanded Cameron.

'About forty minutes. You're thinking of going after him?' said Rora, her voice full of concern.

Cameron nodded, starting for the door. 'If he's heading for Fry's lab on foot, I can catch up with him before he reports to his master.'

'It's a plan,' conceded Rora. 'But I don't like it.'

'Apart from Slater, I'm the only one fast enough to catch him,' Cameron replied. 'And he can't come.'

Slater bristled. 'Why not?'

'We need you here. You know what we have to do, don't you, Rora?'

'What?' Slater looked confused.

'We have to get ready to evacuate,' said Cameron. 'In case I can't stop him in time.'

Rora's eyes were big and wide. She suddenly looked a lot younger than her fifteen years.

'Cameron, don't,' she whispered. 'It's too dangerous. Let's just go now.'

Cameron shook his head.

'I can't leave Darren. He didn't deserve any of this – he probably didn't even know what he was doing. But once he's given Fry the location of the base, he's done his job. Fry won't need him any more. And we all know what happens when Fry's subjects outlive their usefulness.'

'I'll come with you,' said Rora.

'You can't keep up with me. Not all that way. Besides, you're the leader. Your place is here. This is something I have to do.'

Rora grabbed one of Cameron's hands in both of hers. Her bottom lip was trembling, but she nodded firmly. 'Go on then,' she said. 'But you'd better come back.'

She held his gaze for a moment, then turned to Slater. 'Right, get everyone up and assembled in the rec room in five minutes. Tinker, tell Robbie to get the truck ready. Smarts . . .'

Cameron felt a strange, unfamiliar sensation in the pit of his stomach as he watched Rora going back to the business of being leader. But he couldn't quite work out what it was, and there was no time to try to pin it down. He had urgent business of his own.

He had to go and hunt down his best-friend-turned-traitor.

chapter twenty-four

race against time

Darren's trail wasn't hard to follow. Close to the entrance of the base, a narrow path through the thick grass was trampled flat. Cameron didn't need his built-in compass to tell him which direction it was heading.

East.

Towards Fry's laboratory.

Cameron raced forward. He tried to keep out of sight of roads where possible, but the time for concealment was over. What mattered now was speed, and he pushed his patchwork body to its limits in the search for it. The wind whistled in his ears as he sprinted along, faster than a racehorse, his enhanced vision picking up each new sign of Darren's passing – a broken branch here, a muddy footprint there.

The trail veered from side to side, as if Darren had been stumbling and crashing along like an out-of-control vehicle. That gave Cameron some hope. His own straight line was faster and, he thought as he hurdled a dry stone wall, if he didn't have to worry about such obstacles, he could make up some vital ground. Forty minutes was a heck of a head start. But, thanks to Dr Fry, Cameron thought he might just be fast enough.

A chime on his communicator told him that the base was calling.

'Yeah?' he said.

'It's T-T-Tinker,' stammered a familiar voice.

'I'm kind of busy, Tink,' Cameron panted. Even for his cybernetic muscles, maintaining this relentless pace was an effort.

'I k-k-know, but I've thought of something. If Fry is using a Trojan to control Darren, you won't be able to r-r-reason with him. You'll have to f-f-fight him.'

'I'll do whatever I have to do to stop him,'

replied Cameron. 'You don't have to worry about that.'

'Stop talking and *listen to me*!' Tinker's voice was so commanding that Cameron almost stumbled with surprise.

'OK, I'm listening.'

'Without knowing h-h-how the Trojan works, I can't work out a specific c-c-counter-code, but Smarts has had an idea. I'm p-putting him on.'

There was a slight pause, and then Smarts's high-pitched voice sounded in Cameron's ears.

'OK, Cameron,' he said. 'We know that Fry has suppressed Darren's memories of the fire and his mum's death. I think he might have had to do that because Darren's emotions were too powerful for even Fry to control. If we can unlock that power, it might just be enough to break Fry's hold on him. I've designed a very basic programme to boost Darren's memory. Hopefully it should be enough to break down whatever blocks Fry has put up in his mind. Even if it only works temporarily, it should last long enough for you to grab Darren. Tinker's transmitting it now.'

Another chime sounded, and a tiny icon appeared at the bottom of Cameron's HUD.

'I'm sorry but I h-h-haven't had time to get it to work wirelessly,' said Tinker. 'You'll need to c-c-connect directly with one of the implants behind his ears to t-t-transfer the code.'

'Thanks, guys,' replied Cameron. 'I'll let you know how it goes.'

'G-g-good luck.'

The communication ended. Cameron ran on, feeling more confident with every stride. He hadn't had time to think how he would stop Darren if he was still under Fry's control. Now at least he had a chance.

And Tinker's call had reminded him of someone else he needed to speak to. Calling up the number on his HUD, he dialled.

'Jack Austin.'

'It's Cameron. Listen, I don't have a lot of time. You were right about Darren.'

'What's happened?'

'Fry is controlling him. I'm on my way to the lab now. I . . .' Cameron's voice trailed off. 'I'm sorry. I have to go.'

'Wait—'

Cameron cut the call short. He had just come over the low ridge that backed onto Fry's lab complex. Beneath him, a few hundred metres away, a small figure was scrabbling and stumbling across the uneven ground towards the fence.

'Darren!'

Darren spun round as though he'd been hit by a bullet.

Steadying himself, he stared back at Cameron as he marched down the slope. Cameron was still several metres away when he remembered what Tinker had said – he had to be able to connect with Darren to use Smarts's 'cure code'.

But how close would his friend allow him to get?

'Hi, Darren.'

Darren stared back at him. His eyes were cold, no spark of recognition in them at all. He was like a zombie. Cameron wondered whether Fry was watching him through those dead eyes at that very moment. He took another step closer.

'Darren – it's me, Cameron.'

The eyes narrowed. Darren clenched the fist of his unbroken arm. Cameron froze.

'Don't you remember me, mate? I'm Cameron.'

'Cameron?' said Darren. He swayed slightly and tilted his head as though he was having trouble focusing. His knees seemed to give way, and for a moment Cameron thought he was going to pass out. Then, without any warning, Darren sprang towards him. Cameron side-stepped, but he wasn't quite quick enough. Darren's shoulder caught him in the stomach, sending them both tumbling to the ground.

Cameron tried to roll away, but Darren locked an arm around his throat. He was strong – too strong to be normal. Fry had obviously done more than take control of Darren's body. He had somehow boosted his strength too.

Wrenching hard on the choking arm, Cameron just managed to yank it away. Pushing Darren backwards, he jumped clear and assumed a defensive stance. Even with this newfound strength, if it came down to a fight he should be able take Darren, but that wasn't the way Cameron wanted this to play out.

'Listen to me, Darren . . .' Cameron raised his hands. 'Fry is controlling you. He's messed with your memories, but I can help you.'

Darren was up on his feet, fists bunched. His face showed no sign that he could even hear what Cameron was saying. With a snarl, he rushed at him again.

This time, Cameron's side-step was perfectly timed. Dodging Darren's thrown punch, he grabbed him and turned him round in a wrestling hold. One arm locked securely around Darren's chest, he quickly moved his other hand up to his friend's head, locating one of the ports that Fry had installed there. Plugging his data jack into the port, holding

Darren still, he activated Smarts's code.

His own sensors screamed as a burst of data blossomed around him. It felt like a thousand voices all calling his name at once, in a hundred different languages. He staggered, barely able to keep his feet.

The effect on Darren was even more dramatic. He threw his hands up to his ears, as if he could block out the flood of information. Then his knees buckled, and only Cameron's bear-hug prevented him from crumpling to the ground.

Lurching forward with a grunt, Cameron swept Darren up in his good arm, careful not to break the connection. Darren felt as light as a feather. As Cameron looked down, his eyes fluttered open. He stared at Cameron for a moment. Then he spoke.

'I remember.'

Suddenly, thoughts and memories whirled into Cameron's mind.

Memories that were not his own.

Choking black smoke and roaring flames. Desperation as he tried to battle through the heat to his mum's room. The horrible realization that he couldn't get there. Darkness. Waking up in an unfamiliar bed. Doctors. Nurses. Bandages. Pain. Pain everywhere. And a sad voice. 'I'm sorry, son. I'm afraid your mother is dead . . .'

All the emotions that had been pent up by Dr Fry were released from Darren with the force of a dam bursting – the grief, the loss, the anger, Cameron felt them all, as if he had actually lived through them.

Then, as suddenly as it had begun, the flow of memories ended. Darren lay still in Cameron's arms, limp and broken, like he'd been hit by a truck. As Cameron carefully broke the connection between them, Darren opened his mouth to speak but no words came out. He tried again. Finally he drew a shuddering breath.

'Cam . . .'

'I'm sorry, Darren,' murmured Cameron. 'I'm so, so sorry.'

''Bout what?'

'For all this. If you hadn't helped me, none

of it would have happened.'

Darren's face cracked into a tired grin.

'Don't be daft,' he said. 'Fry came to our house before you even called that day. He blackmailed me. That's got nothing to do with you. I *chose* to help you because I'm your friend. Fry did what he did because he's a psycho. It's not your fault.'

Cameron couldn't believe how good those four small words sounded.

'Let's get you out of here,' he said.

'You took the words right out of my mouth.'

Darren smiled. Then suddenly his smile contorted into a grimace and his eyes rolled up. His head jerked back and his whole body shook.

'Darren! What is it?' demanded Cameron, panicking. Had the cure code damaged something? '*Darren!*'

There was no answer. With a final convulsive shudder, Darren slid out of his arms and crumpled to the ground.

Cameron dropped to his knees beside him.

'Darren!'

Darren's eyes fluttered open for a moment, but they seemed to be staring past Cameron, flicking from side to side, filled with shock and confusion.

'Cam . . .' he croaked. 'Look . . .'

Then his eyes turned glassy and still. Cameron felt for a pulse at his best friend's neck. Nothing.

Darren was dead.

'How tragic,' said a chill, unfeeling voice.

Cameron looked up. Standing just beyond the fence was the tall figure of Dr Lazarus Fry.

In his hand he held a small black box.

On his face he wore the shark-like smile of a killer.

chapter twenty-five

the judas code

Fry lowered the control device. Eyes glinting coldly behind his glasses, he allowed his icy smile to spread. It was one of the ugliest expressions Cameron had ever seen.

'Such a waste,' he remarked. 'But when using unreliable servants, I find it's always best to build in a self-destruct mechanism.'

Cameron felt a wave of hate churning inside him. The fact that Fry was gloating made him sick to his stomach. It was bad enough that he could steal the life of his best friend at the press of a button. To celebrate the fact was pure evil.

'If only you'd thought to fit me with one of those,' said Cameron grimly.

He stepped over Darren's lifeless body and headed towards the fence. Fry stood his ground, but maybe he couldn't see the murderous intent in Cameron's eye. All Cameron wanted to do was tear down the fence and start punching Fry's face with the mechanical fist the doctor had equipped him with. Nothing he did now could bring Darren back, but it would be the closest thing to justice he could mete out. The only justice Fry deserved.

'Yeah,' he continued. 'I bet you're really regretting that now. You should have kitted me out with an off-switch as well as all this other gear.' He flexed his machine-arm, allowing Fry a good look at his own handiwork. 'That's a mistake that's going to cost you.'

'Well, it's impossible to think of everything in advance,' confessed Fry with a shrug. 'Although I flatter myself I did quite a reasonable job on this occasion.'

He tucked the device in his pocket and clasped his hands behind his back. Cameron was at the fence now, but something in the back of his mind was warning him to hold off. Fry was too cocky – too confident for an unarmed man facing a murderous opponent. He had another trick up the sleeve of his white lab coat, Cameron was sure of it.

'Of course, I couldn't have done it without you,' continued Fry. 'The enhancements you're showing off are courtesy of my genius, but your predictability is all your own. You have performed admirably.'

'What do you mean, performed?'

Fry smiled. 'There are many kinds of puppet, my young Pinocchio. There are those we work by wires' – he gestured behind Cameron towards Darren's still body – 'and then there are those like you – who would swear they were acting entirely on their own instincts, but in actual fact have done everything that their puppeteer has desired.'

'I'm not your puppet,' Cameron growled.

'Really?' Fry arched an eyebrow in fake surprise. 'And yet you broke into my laboratory, exactly as I wanted. You rescued your poor – late – friend there, exactly as I wanted, and took him into your secret base. The place even I could never find. Didn't you think it was just a little *too* convenient, the way you found Darren so easily? But what am I saying? Of course you didn't. You were too blinded by the delusion of your own brilliance and daring.'

Cameron stared, disbelieving. 'It was a setup? Right from the start?'

'I suppose that depends on where you consider the start to be. But yes, from a very early stage.'

Cameron shook his head. There was no way he was going to accept that he had been played so thoroughly.

'Wait . . . No, that's not possible. I didn't even find out that you had Darren until I went to the hospital. And I wouldn't have gone there unless—' He stopped himself. There was no point letting Fry know that one of the Republic's monsters had been shot. It was a potential weakness he might exploit. 'Unless there was something we needed. And you couldn't have predicted that.'

Fry stepped closer to the fence, taunting Cameron with his proximity.

'Oh, but I didn't have to. I knew that you would try to find him sooner or later. Your misplaced sense of loyalty would drive you to it. The exact route isn't important as long as the destination is the same. And we've already arrived.'

'Arrived? Where?'

'Where the Judas Code was designed to lead. The end. The end of the so-called Monster Republic.'

Cameron froze. Fry's triumphant face was so close he could have punched it through the fence. But the doctor was still just too confident. And what he was saying didn't make sense.

'Judas Code? That's what you were using to control Darren? Tinker said it was a Trojan horse.'

Dr Fry shrugged. 'Ah, well. Perhaps he should have spent a little less time with his nose in electronics manuals and a little more reading the Bible. If he had, he might have known that although the authorities may try to bring you down, in the end it's always your friends who betray you.'

'Darren didn't betray me,' snarled Cameron. 'You *forced* him do what he did. He had no choice. And I know what you were trying to do – you wanted to bring Darren here so he could lead you back to the Republic. But we stopped you. We broke your Judas Code. Darren never told you where our base is.'

Fry sneered. 'Still so ploddingly short-sighted, Cameron. I didn't need Darren to tell me anything. Once the Judas Code was activated, it triggered a hidden tracking device. It wouldn't have shown up in any scans before that – it was operating as a harmless data processor, with a number of apparently redundant components built in. But as soon as the Judas Code was up and running, those components went to work – busily transmitting the location of your "secret" base.'

Cameron shook his head. It didn't make sense. 'Then why did you want Darren back here?'

'I didn't. He was a lure. His final function

was to bring *you* here. The ultimate betrayal – to make sure you were out of the way when the Bloodhounds arrived at your base.' Fry smiled and made a show of examining his watch. 'Which would be right about now.'

Rora paced the control room, casting anxious glances at the monitor screens. Since Tinker had sent the 'cure code' there had been no word from Cameron. Had he caught up with Darren, or had Fry's unwitting agent made it back to the lab ahead of him? Was Cameron walking into a trap?

Too many questions and no answers.

The base felt empty without Cameron. He had been gone too long and too often lately. The fact that Rora hadn't approved of all those expeditions didn't alter the fact that she missed him. Each and every time. She had tried to tell herself it was because she had grown used to having him around, but that wasn't it. Slater had been part of her life for longer, but she often tired of his company. With Cameron, even when they were arguing, part of Rora knew that they would always make up later. Now she was all too aware that he was going into danger from which he might not return. She hadn't even had time to apologize for her mistake in blaming Austin for Darren's sabotage. She wished Cameron would hurry back so she could say sorry.

'Come on,' she muttered to the empty room, glancing at the blank screens for the hundredth time. Couldn't he at least report in? He must know she'd be fretting about him.

Suddenly a light on the console next to the monitors flashed on in a steady, even blink.

Rora smiled. That light meant that someone was approaching the main entrance. Her heart leaped. Even if Darren had made it back to the lab, there was no way Fry's minions could have made it here so soon. It had to be Cameron! He must have caught up with his friend and was bringing him back in.

Rora flew to the door. It was reckless – she knew she should stay at her post – but Cameron had saved the Republic; he deserved a hero's welcome. Maybe even a hug . . .

She ran up the sloping tunnel. Owl was sitting upright and alert at Guard's station. His surveillance capabilities were nowhere near as advanced as Guard's, but now the threat of Darren revealing their location was gone, he was more than good enough for the job.

'Hey, Owl,' she said. 'Cameron's coming in. I think he's got Darren.'

'Thank God,' breathed Owl.

'Yeah. Could you run down and tell Slater to put a hold on the evacuation?'

'Sure.' Owl nodded and scampered back down into the base.

As she strode out into the fresh air, Rora wondered whether Cameron would make something of the fact she was out here waiting for him. Well, if he did, she'd just tell him she was stretching her legs. Smiling to herself, she took a moment to cast her gaze over the landscape. The mountains had always struck her as rather bleak and desolate, but now the low morning sun painted the hillside a rich, beautiful gold. Perhaps it had been her worries colouring everything grey.

She wished Cameron would hurry up. She had a hundred and one things to attend to and she couldn't afford to waste too much time waiting out here. At last she spotted movement slightly further down the hill, and heard the heavy tramp of footsteps.

Too heavy.

Rora frowned. Cameron's machine-powered footsteps were pretty thunderous, but these sounded even louder. Maybe he was carrying Darren? Her first instinct was to duck back into the tunnel to check the monitors, but she told herself she was just edgy. Instead, she advanced a short way for a better view down the hillside. A moment later, a figure emerged over the nearest ridge.

But the figure she saw was too bulky, its shoulders too hunched to be Cameron. It skirted a rocky outcrop and kept on coming. It was headed straight for the tunnel entrance. Straight for her.

It was a Bloodhound.

With her insides turning to solid ice, Rora scanned for signs of others. Sure enough, there were more emerging into view, low to the ground, loping up the hill on all fours, sunlight glinting off their cruel metal teeth. And now, above them, wheeling in the clear blue sky, her sharp eyes picked out the winged shapes of Bloodhawks. Dozens of them.

This was no search party. This was a concerted attack.

And the base was blind. She'd left the control room empty. She'd sent Owl to find Slater. Nobody knew they were coming except her.

Rora started to back away, trembling. But before she could turn and run for the tunnel, her eye was caught by a new shape moving up in the wake of the advancing pack, darker and more fearsome than any Bloodhound.

It was about twice the size, its already intimidating frame bulked out with spiked black armour. A monstrous wolf-head was mounted on hunched shoulders, its jaws lined with savage steel teeth. In addition to great mechanical claws, its powerful arms bristled with weaponry. Gun-barrels that made Cameron's net-launcher look like a water pistol were clustered around its forearms and fixed to its shoulders. Its eyes blazed a bloody red as it stalked up the hill.

For a terrifying moment the giant monster robbed Rora of the power to move. Then, throwing back its head, the creature let out a hideous howl that echoed off the rocks of the mountainside like the sound of the end of the world.

Jolted into action, Rora ran for the tunnel, desperate to reach Guard's station and sound the general alarm.

Praying it wasn't already too late.

chapter twenty-six

ashes to ashes

Cameron smashed his arm against the fence and roared his frustration at Fry. The doctor stood his ground, saying nothing, the cruel smile still fixed on his face. Cameron would have loved to wipe it off but he didn't have time, and Fry knew it.

Frantic, Cameron spun round and raced away, leaving behind the lab, Dr Fry – even Darren's body – thinking only of the Republic and his friends. As he ran, he summoned up the communicator on his HUD and began hailing the base.

'Rora? Come in! Tinker? Anyone! Come in!'

But all he got was static. The channel was dead.

He ran on, faster. The terrain rushed past in a blur. He pushed himself on and on, powering his legs with every scrap of energy he had. He scrabbled up slopes and threw himself down the other side.

'Somebody answer!' he yelled.

The static hissed back at him.

Then it crackled and a voice broke in.

'Cameron!'

'Rora! Thank God! I—'

'Cameron, listen! Stay clear! Whatever you do, don't come back here!'

'Rora! What're you talking about? I'm on my way right now!'

Rora's answer was drowned out by more hisses and crackles. When she came through again, she was shouting to make herself heard above a growing din in the background. Screams, gunshots and explosions underlined her every word.

'They're here, Cameron! The Bloodhounds! Stay away! There are too many . . .' Gunfire rattled violently across her next words. It sounded deafeningly close. '. . . find you if we can get out. We'll—'

The channel went dead.

As horrifying as the noise of battle had been, the silence ringing in Cameron's ears was a hundred times worse.

'*RORA!*'

Disobeying her orders once again, he carried on running flat out for the base. He'd fallen for Fry's deception. He'd left his friends at the mercy of the Bloodhounds – left Freddy, Tinker, *Rora* . . .

With a roar of fury, Cameron ran on, into the unknown.

The entrance tunnel was deserted.

Guard's security post was a smoking ruin, the smashed monitors still sparking feebly in the gloom. Cameron raced past. There had been no sign of enemies on the slopes outside, but that didn't mean they weren't lurking below. But there was no time for caution now.

Maybe Rora had managed to evacuate,

Cameron told himself. Maybe what he had heard had been the sound of a fighting withdrawal.

The thin hope dissipated as he advanced into what was left of the base. It was a war zone. Smoke drifted along the corridors. Great gouges had been torn in the walls, like the claw-marks of some prehistoric beast. Conduits and cables had been ripped free. Lines of bullet holes pockmarked the roof and floor. Tinker's workshop was a scene of total devastation, all the equipment and his lovingly restored and customized dentist's chair smashed to pieces. The body of a Bloodhound lay sprawled amongst the mess . . .

Cameron's heart skipped a beat.

It wasn't a Bloodhound. It was Guard.

Cameron knelt down beside the broken figure, but he already knew there was nothing he could do. Guard's neck was bent at an unnatural angle, his small body cold and still. Already injured by Darren, he would have had no chance when the Bloodhounds burst in. The thought of Fry's killers attacking the helpless young monster made Cameron sick to the stomach.

Saying a silent goodbye, he ducked back out again and carried on towards the control room. A few Bloodhound bodies were strewn along the corridor, one lying slumped beneath the still form of another familiar monster.

Cameron swallowed. This time it was Rehana, the girl with the reptilian skin. Her high cheekbones were stained with blood, the marks of teeth clear across her shoulder and arm. Another casualty of Fry's attack on the Republic.

He moved on. The door to the control room had been ripped off its hinges, revealing a barrier formed of tables, chairs and banks of machinery. It hadn't stopped the Bloodhounds. Beyond the makeshift barricade, the room was even more of a wreck than the rest of the base. The worst of the battle had taken place right here. Everything inside had been pulverized or blown apart. The consoles were raked with bullet holes. Cameron knew the Republic had no weapons capable of such a volume of gunfire.

He also knew there was no way out.

He advanced further into the room, sifting through the wreckage, kicking aside the trashed furniture, searching for something, although he had no idea what. There was blood everywhere – spattered over stretches of wall and smeared across the floor – but of Rora the room gave him no sign.

This had been where she had made her last stand, though, Cameron was certain of it. Trapped, cornered, she had tried to warn him to keep away even while the Bloodhounds were tearing their way inside. He hung his head, tears threatening to overwhelm him.

Had all the others been here too? Smarts, Tinker and the rest? Had anyone managed to get out? He'd seen only two dead bodies, but that didn't mean the others had escaped. More likely they had been taken back to Fry's lab – the one place they all feared above all others.

There was still much more of the base left to search, but Cameron sagged, not sure if he had the energy. At the same time, he knew he had to try. There was no one else. He turned slowly, bracing himself for the task ahead.

To find his path barred by a tall, muscular figure that seemed to fill the doorway. The sharp features were black with smoke and blood, but there was no mistaking the eyes, nor their gaze of undisguised hatred.

Slater.

Slater advanced into the room, surveying the devastation impassively. Scuttling in behind him came Crawler, followed by a girl with mousy brown hair, cat-like eyes and blades protruding from her forearms. She had escaped from the lab before Fry could program her as a warrior, however, so although in looks she lived up to her nickname of Deadly, she usually steered clear of fighting. This time, it was clear, no one had had that luxury. Still, Deadly seemed to have survived the battle with nothing worse than a bloodied lip and several cuts to her cheek and brow.

Slater eyed Cameron. 'I thought I'd find you sniffing around here.'

'I came back as quickly as I could,' said Cameron, hoping they could set aside their dislike for now. 'What happened? Where's Rora?'

Slater gestured around the room. 'What happened? We got pasted. Fry threw something new at us. They called it a Warhound – like a giant Bloodhound but with built-in guns and a shoulder-mounted rocket-launcher. Where's Rora? It took her. Along with Owl and Digger and most of the others.'

'Come on then!' said Cameron, starting past Slater. 'We have to go after them!'

Slater threw an arm out, blocking him.

'*We?* You just don't get it, do you?' he spat. 'There is no "we" any more. It's over! The Republic's finished! I've collected as many survivors as I can find. We're setting up our own group, and you're not invited. That way, *we* might stand a chance.'

Cameron's lip curled in disdain. Inside he was shaking with anger.

'Right, that figures. So what's this group of yours going to be called? The Monster Monarchy?

With you on the throne, I suppose?'

'Yeah, very funny.' Slater gestured at his battle-scarred henchmen. 'Do you see anyone laughing?'

Nobody was. Their faces were grim and their eyes held only contempt and the promise of violence. If Crawler and Deadly were an indication of the sort of monsters who had rallied to Slater's banner, then he had picked his team well. These survivors were definitely on his side.

'Democracy's overrated anyway,' said Slater. 'Every time we put anything to one of your votes, somebody gets hurt and the Republic ends up in deeper trouble. The marina, the lab, the journalist – you make a pretty speech and we all risk our lives to go along with what you want to do.'

Cameron opened his mouth to argue, but Slater wasn't about to give him the chance to speak.

'Well, this isn't a popularity contest any more. This is survival. Whatever we are, we'll be looking out for ourselves and watching each other's backs. And you? You get what you wanted all along – to be leader of the Monster Republic. A republic of one.' He laughed bitterly. 'I only came back here to see if there was anything worth salvaging. And guess what? There isn't.'

Slater spun on his heel and nodded to his two lieutenants. 'Come on.'

They marched off without another word. Cameron watched them go in stunned silence. There had been times when he had thought of leaving the Republic. But he had never thought *it* would leave *him*.

Sinking to his knees amid the devastation, he tried to clear his head and decide what to do. If Rora had been taken alive, there was only one possible place Fry would be keeping her. The laboratory. He had to go back. It didn't matter that he was outnumbered. It was suicide, he knew that. But he couldn't abandon Rora and who knew how many others to torture and death at the hands of their greatest enemy.

Besides, what was there left to live for?

'C-C-Cameron?'

Cameron raised his head. Peering into the room through cracked glasses, spiky hair grubby and dust-streaked, was a timid, tear-stained face.

'Tinker!'

Cameron was on his feet and at the door in an instant. He couldn't believe his eyes. The narrow corridor was filled with monsters. He saw Freddy, with Jace propped up against his shoulder, along with eight or ten others. With their slumped, defeated looks they were a pitiful handful, but they were alive. At their head, Tinker was gently cradling a small body in his gangly arms.

At first, Cameron didn't realize who it was. The pale features were familiar, but he didn't recognize the eyes. They were such a bright, vivid blue that he couldn't understand why he didn't remember them.

Unless he hadn't seen them before. Unless they were usually hidden behind a pair of large dark glasses . . .

'Oh no,' he said, his voice no more than a

whisper.

Tinker's head twitched convulsively. 'He was still in the w-w-workshop with Guard when the Bloodhounds came in. I tried to get down to him, but there was n-n-no way through. They must have caught him and—' His voice choked off, fresh tears rolling down his cheeks.

Cameron gently brushed his human fingers across Smarts's face. With his eyes closed, the boy looked as if he was sleeping. Cameron couldn't believe that he would never hear his cheerful voice again. Smarts had been his first friend in the Republic. Now he was gone, along with who knew how many others.

Cameron laid a consoling hand on Tinker's shoulder. 'It's not your fault, OK?' he said hoarsely. He looked around at the pathetic gathering. Almost without exception, they were the youngest and least able-bodied Rejects. 'None of you could have held off an attack like that.'

'We managed to hide in the lower tunnels,' said Freddy. 'They didn't come down that far.'

'Are there any more of you?'

Freddy shook his head. 'Some of the others managed to hide too. They came out when the Bloodhounds had gone, but then Slater came back. He said he was starting up a new group. But he was only interested in Robbie and Tinker and the other strong ones. He didn't want the rest of us. He took Robbie. He didn't want to go, but Slater made him.'

'B-b-but he d-didn't f-find me!' said Tinker defiantly.

Cameron sighed. He could well imagine Slater trying to press-gang Tinker into his new outfit. It made sense. The Republic had relied heavily on his technical wizardry. They'd relied on Smarts too. Divided, the monsters were going to have a harder future ahead.

'What were you thinking of doing?'

'There's an old factory we used as a safe house once before,' said Freddy. 'We figured we'd set up there for the time being. Until we find somewhere else.'

Cameron nodded.

'W-w-will you c-c-come with us?' asked

Tinker. The fear and desperation in his voice tore at Cameron's heart.

'Sure,' he said, forcing the words past the lump in his throat. 'We need to stick together. Now more than ever. But listen, I have to do something first. You go ahead and I'll catch up. Take anything you think might be useful, but don't load yourselves down too much.'

'There might be food in the stores,' suggested Jace. 'I don't think the Bloodhounds smashed those up and Slater might not have taken everything.'

'Good,' said Cameron. 'Check it out. But don't take too long.'

He turned to leave.

'Where are you g-going?'

Cameron stopped and faced Tinker.

'The Bloodhounds took Rora and the others. I'm going to try to get them back. The more the merrier, right?'

Tinker smiled sadly. 'R-r-right.'

chapter twenty-seven

the end of the line

Darren's body had gone.

That was the first thing Cameron noticed when he arrived at the laboratory. With a jolt, he realized that he hadn't even had time to grieve for his best friend. There would be time for that later.

Once he had found Rora.

He gazed beyond the spot where Darren had died in his arms, and knew instantly that something was wrong. Fry must have been expecting him. The place should have been bristling with guards and Bloodhounds. But the gates to the compound stood open. There were no guards in sight, and no lights in any of the buildings. The place was like a ghost town.

Tentatively, Cameron walked closer, expecting an ambush at any moment. But there was nothing but the low moan of the wind. He passed unchallenged through the gates. Marching across the yard to the main building, he shattered the glass sliding door with a single punch.

Nobody came running. There were no alarms. Nothing.

Cameron walked through the deserted corridors of Dr Fry's lair. Every room was silent: laboratories, offices, locker rooms and store cupboards. Not just silent – stripped. Of equipment, personnel, even furniture.

Fry had cleared out.

This was no hurried evacuation. The operation must have been meticulously planned. It was probably finished even before Fry had taunted Cameron over Darren's dead body. With an ever-sinking heart, Cameron searched on, feeling as desolate as the building whose lonely corridors he haunted.

The only sign that the place had ever been inhabited was a row of cages along the wall of one large room. Cameron walked up to the bars. The cages were bolted to the floor. Probably more trouble than they were worth to remove. They were all empty.

Cameron drew a deep breath. He could search every room in the whole complex, but deep down he knew it would be useless. Perhaps Slater had been wrong, and the Warhound hadn't captured Rora at all. Perhaps she was dead, lying somewhere among the wreckage of the base.

All he knew for certain was that she wasn't here.

As he turned to go, Cameron caught sight of something on the floor of the end cage. A flash of colour in a distinctive, unmistakable shade.

His heart leaped to his throat.

Pushing the cage door open, he stepped inside and stooped to pick up the small clump of auburn hairs.

Fox fur.

Cameron shut his eyes tight. She had been here. But now she was gone – and he had no idea where to find her.

Cameron didn't know how long he stood in the cage before the sound of footsteps brought him back to himself. He didn't look up. There was only one person it could be.

'There's nothing left, is there?' said Jack Austin. 'He's thorough, I'll give him that.'

'What are you doing here?' asked Cameron.

'When you hung up on me, I got in the car and came over. I knew you'd be coming here. What happened?'

Cameron swallowed and took a deep breath. He hardly knew where to begin. He rolled the fur between his fingers, feeling its softness, as he filled Austin in on events since they had last spoken – the encounter with Fry, his push-button murder of Darren, the battle at the base. There was no sense in secrecy now. He told him everything.

'What will you do next?' asked Austin gently when Cameron reached the end of his tale.

Cameron closed his human eye for an instant and his human fingers tightened on the fine auburn hairs.

'I'm going to find Rora and the others – I'm going to get them back. And I'm going to make Fry pay for everything he's done – to Marie, to Darren, to all of us.'

'Well, good,' said Austin. 'That sounds like something I can help you with.'

Cameron looked the man in the eye. 'Really?'

'Really.'

From somewhere beyond his anger and pain, Cameron produced a smile. It felt good to have an ally.

'Can I start by giving you a lift somewhere?'

Cameron nodded.

'Back to Broad Harbour,' he said. 'There are some friends I'd like you to meet.'

MONSTER REPUBLIC

by Ben Horton

An explosion in a nuclear power plant.
Kids patched up with scavenged body parts
and bionic implants. A growing army of superhuman
soldiers programmed for destruction.

Cameron Riley is about to discover that
what doesn't kill you makes you stronger . . .

ISBN: 978 0 552 55870 9

CRAWLERS

by Sam Enthoven

They will do anything for their Queen
– and soon, so will you . . .

Four boys and four girls are on a
trip to the theatre. Little do they know
that they will never see the play. They're
about to be plunged into a nightmare.
Beneath the theatre lies a secret.
And now she has been released . . .

ISBN: 978 0 552 558709

*Hellish demons, vomiting bats, world-class martial arts –
what more do you want in a book?*

THE BLACK TATTOO
By **SAM ENTHOVEN**

The creature had reared up in
its true form, a frozen man-sized
explosion of pink custard-like stuff. It
wobbled and shook. Big bubbles
formed and popped on its skin,
belching out words.

'Fresh meat!' it burped. 'Fresh meat! Fresh meat!'

'Whatever,' said Jack – and sighed. *Yep*, he thought. *Gang up
on the new guy.* In some ways, when it came down to it,
Hell was really pretty predictable . . .

**'Sam Enthoven's clearly loving telling this story and
his energy creeps into the words on every page'**
Philip Ardagh, *Guardian*

'I think Sam could be the next Anthony Horowitz'
Charlie, 11

ISBN: 978 0 552 55358 2

Z.REX

by Steve Cole

You're a thirteen-year-old boy on the run.

A massive, man-eating dinosaur is after you.

Evil scientists want you both dead.

There's only one way out.

You and the monster have to work together . . .

ISBN: 978 1 862 30777 3

Z.RAPTOR
by Steve Cole

Caught in a real-life game – where the only law is survival.
Adam thought it was all over.

He thought he and his dad had escaped.
That they had left the monsters far behind.
That they were safe.

Now, Adam is trapped on a tiny Pacific island.
There is no food, no phone, and no way out. And he is being
hunted by vicious packs of hyper-evolved dinosaurs with a
human's ability to learn . . . and a beast's ability to kill.

ISBN: 978 1 862 30778 0